The Enchantment of Big Canoe

Other Books by Carl Japikse:

The Super Unofficial Atlanta Souvenir Guide
Pigging Out in Columbus
Teeing Off in Central Ohio

Love Virtue
The Light Within Us
The Fabled Gate

Making the Right Things Happen
The Enlightened Management Journal

The $1.98 Cookbook
The Biggest Tax Cheat in America is the I.R.S.

It's All in the Mind
The Hour Glass

As Waldo Japussy:
The Tao of Meow
The Ruby Cat of Waldo Japussy

As Editor:
Sophy, The Journal of Inspired Writing
The Sinew of America
Patriot Dream
The Poems of Light

The Enchantment
of Big Canoe

by Carl Japikse

THE PIERIAN SPRING
Big Canoe, Georgia

Special thanks to—
Paul Hanks, Tina Perry,
Debbie Pickett, Jeff Dussault,
and Chiquita Berry

THE ENCHANTMENT OF BIG CANOE
Copyright © 2000 by Carl Japikse

All Rights Reserved. No part of this book may be used or re-produced in any manner whatsoever without written permission, except in the case of brief quotations embodied in reviews and articles. Printed in the United States of America. Direct inquiries to the Pierian Spring, P.O. Box 271, Marble Hill, GA 30148.

ISBN 0-89804-700-5

Table of Contents

The Enchantment of Big Canoe

The Enchanted Land

It is clear the moment you first drive in the main gate. There is something magical about this land. It's the mountains—but more than the mountains. It's the gurgling streams and serene lakes—but more than the streams and lakes. It's the sunlight dappling the leaves of the trees. It's the graceful loping of white-tailed deer as they romp through the woods; the proud march of a gaggle of geese along the bank of Lake Petit or a flock of wild turkeys as they "promenande right." It's the crunch of leaves and acorns and tiny branches under your feet as you walk along a trail. It's the moss and ferns lining the marshes and creeks. It's the hawks soaring overhead. It's the ravines and coves, each one a miniature hermitage. It's the holiness of the occasional meadow, bowed under the arching ceiling of the surrounding woods. It's the excitement of discovering an old rock chimney and foundation, the remaining ruins of courageous pioneers and settlers who were drawn to live here hundreds of years ago.

But it's more than all of these delights—even all of them put together. As you walk along the trails throughout Big Canoe, you half expect to see sylphs flitting through the air, or elves dancing on the tops of mushrooms. What's that? Did you hear it? It almost sounded like the pipes of Pan being played—

Enchantment sings from daffodils in spring

8

Enchantment clings to the trees after an ice storm

just over there.   No, it wasn't just the whistling of the wind.

There is a definite charm in the air—an allurement that defies explanation.   It cannot be seen, but it speaks to everyone, each in his or her own way.

Perhaps it is a legacy of the many Indian peoples who lived in this region long before Big Canoe first opened its gates. One group left us the mystery of the rock cairns, estimated to be 4,000 to 6,000 year old.   Did they leave a spell as well?

It is less likely that the charm was left by early settlers like the Disharoons.   But they may have left their belief in it.

That's what the current "settlers" of Big Canoe are doing, too. We perpetuate the charm by believing in it enough to move here and make this mountain woods our home, too.   The enchantment enters our hearts and minds and becomes a part of our inner makeup, our innate essence, as well.

At any rate, it was the Indians who first recognized the spell of these North Georgia woods.   They called it "the enchanted land."

Part of the enchantment is surely the quiet and the calmness of these woods.   Throughout Big Canoe, a new dimension of serenity and peace is only a few steps from anyone's front door.

9

Reminders of the past, like these two chimneys from the McElroy cabin, add to the allure of Big Canoe

Some people find it in a boat or canoe, floating lazily on Lake Pettit. Others find it in special places where they can sit alongside a stream or tiny pool in the woods, letting nature renew them and temporarily shelter them from the stresses and demands of daily life.

It is sometimes hard to believe that a woodland that can touch the deepest spirit within us can be so close to Atlanta. It is not just an escape—it is a transformation.

The enchantment of Big Canoe enriches life. This is not an allurement of Sirens to be resisted. It is a force that welcomes you and makes you feel as though you have come home at last. It extends comfort and hospitality. It embraces you and makes you a part of the spell. It fills you with new vigor, new ideas, and a new zest.

Big Canoe is less than 30 years old. At first, it was primarily a getaway for folks toiling in Atlanta. But as it has matured, a strong sense of community is developing as well—and this, too, is part of the charm. The residents have a common bond—they all love the mountain woods. They have all been touched by the charm and power of their chosen home. They recognize it in one another.

Life in Big Canoe is a celebration of this enchantment.

They Say It Best

The best testimony about the enchantment of Big Canoe, of course, is the large number of people who have decided to make it their home. In one case, a husband and wife who had just moved into a new home elsewhere visited friends in Big Canoe. After a few days, the husband announced to his wife: "Honey, we're moving again." And they did! They built yet another new home—in Big Canoe.

Here are other tributes from the people who know Big Canoe the best:

"There are no bad views in Big Canoe. Every view is a great one."—*Bob Turley, resident.*

"There is a spiritual quality about Big Canoe that Dave and I both sensed the first time we visited. That's what inspired us to buy a lot and move here."—*Charlene Terrell, resident.*

"This piece of land has always been beautiful. It's the people—everyone together—that has made Big Canoe a great place to live."—*William Byrne, president of Big Canoe Company.*

"The appreciation of property values in Big Canoe is incredible. I have never seen this kind of increase in value in any other development."—*George Kudrick, former vice-president, Bank of North Georgia, now a builder in Big Canoe.*

"It's a wonderful place, filled with wonderful people."—*Dorothy Haist, resident.*

Visiting Big Canoe

Not everyone is lucky enough to live permanently in Big Canoe—or even own a lot. Some folks visit the enchanted land by the weekend—or the week.

The good news: Big Canoe is set up to welcome them and show them the time of their life.

Visiting Big Canoe is a great way to get to know

A rental customer registers with Tabby Rittenberry

the community—from the inside. It also is a good way for some of Big Canoe's homeowners to make extra money. These are Big Canoeists who have built a home but have still not moved here permanently. They may only use their home a few weekends or weeks throughout the year. So they rent it out to vacationers whenever they are not in residence.

The details are all expertly handled by Ann Young and her team at the Chimneys Conference Center, located next to the General Store in Wolfscratch Village. They match the needs of vacationers to the properties available, book their reservations, and make sure they have a great time during their visit.

Many visitors are vacationing couples and families enjoying the recreational facilities of Big Canoe. Some come for weddings; others come for reunions. Often, two or three families will rent a home big enough to lodge them all, and vacation together. The homes in Big Canoe offer this kind of versatility.

The other major source of visitors staying in Big Canoe are the professionals and business people who come to the Chimneys for a conference. They receive the same courteous and attentive service.

Rental units range from one and two bedroom condos, cabins, and villas in the heart of Big Canoe to four and five bedroom homes with mountain views, tucked away in Big Canoe's neighborhoods. All units come with cable television, full kitchen, deck, and fireplace. Most also feature a grill, video player, microwave, and washer and dryer. A few offer a Jacuzzi tub, screened-in porches, and other features of comfort.

Prices range from $130 a night off season in a condo to $2000 a week for a five-bedroom home during the summer season and holidays. Vacationers staying in Big Canoe can use all of the amenities of the community—golf, tennis, swimming, boating, and fishing—for standard daily fees.

According to Ann, many of the families that vacation in Big Canoe have a long tradition of visiting the Enchanted Land. "Big Canoe is well-known throughout the South as a premier mountain resort. Most folks who come here want to come back. And they do. But we are not satisfied unless *everyone* who vacations with us wants to come back—again and again."

Brenda Stewart and her housekeeping crew—Jessica Artinger and Deanna Hendley—ensure a spotless rental

Lost—or Found?

It is not a simple proposition to build a road in Big Canoe. There are lakes. Roads must go around them. There are also mountains. Roads must snake in between them. The result? A veritable maze of roadways—some 80 miles of it—which wind and wend throughout the 7,600 acres of Big Canoe.

The first time you try to drive unescorted anywhere inside Big Canoe, it is almost guaranteed that you will end up lost. But there are a few simple ways to cope with the confusion.

To start with, one key road runs from the front gate to the north gate, like the spine of the Enchanted Land. This road is aptly named "Wilderness Parkway." If you can find Wilderness Parkway, you can always find your way to a gate.

As you drive into Big Canoe from the front gate, Wilderness Parkway forks with Wolfscratch Road just past the entrance to Sconti clubhouse. Wolfscratch veers right and heads for the heart of the community. Wilderness Parkway goes uphill past the golf course before sweeping by Lake Petit and reuniting with the other end of Wolfscratch.

All other roads lead off of this central network. But every branching is clearly marked with signs. And at the top of each sign, there is a big white arrow.

The arrow is a little like the breadcrumbs in *Hansel and Gretel*. Follow the arrows, and they will lead you back to Wolfscratch Village, the heart of Big Canoe.

Given this basic knowledge, you are ready to explore. The first place to get to know, of course, would be Wolfscratch Village, just to the north of Lake Sconti. Wolfscratch Village consists of the real estate office, the Chimney's conference center, the country store, the post office, and the chapel and Broyles Center. It is a gathering point for the whole community.

The swim and tennis clubs are adjacent to Wolfscratch. In fact, the tennis club occupies the historic Wolfscratch schoolhouse built by the Tates to educate mountain children who lived close by. The swim club is built on the southern edge of Lake Disharoon, which is linked to Lake Sconti by the rock slide.

The golf club and Sconti restaurant are located on the south side of Lake Sconti. All three golf nines—Choctaw, Creek, and Cherokee—radiate outward from the clubhouse, snaking their ways through woods and along side streams and lakes.

Heading north from Wolfscratch leads you to Lake Petit, the venue for boating, canoeing, and fishing. Taking a left will lead you across the dam—if you get a permit from the ducks. Follow Petit Ridge road to Quail Cove Drive and it will lead you to the Indian Rocks Park, one of the most intriguing green areas in Big Canoe. If, instead, you stay on Petit Ridge and take Wake Robin and Columbine to Valley View Drive, you can park and walk to the upper and lower falls in Nature Valley.

As you get off the major thoroughfares, you may notice that the street names are both colorful and natural: Fire Pink, Fallen Deer Path, and Indigo Bunting. In Eagles Landing, it is helpful to know Cherokee, with road names such as Ahaluna Place and Ahyoka Knoll.

If, on the other hand, you do not cross the dam but stay on Wilderness Parkway, you will eventually reach the McDaniel Meadows and the Wildcat Recreation Center, now under construction. If you have toted your bicycles, you can go for a spin on the newly-constructed bike path which starts at the Recreation Center and runs parallel to Wildcat Lane.

Finally, if you go all the way to the North Gate, you will discover where to dump your trash.

15

Living in Big Canoe

People come to Big Canoe from all over the globe. Most of them are refugees from Cobb and Fulton counties, but a surprising number make their way to the Enchanted Land from Ohio, New York, and other non-sacred parts of the country. Some even come from overseas.

At first they come to visit—most likely to spend a vacation or two, or attend a conference at the Chimneys. When they return home, they can't seem to forget the charm and grace of the few days they spent among the mountains. They decide to come back, again and again.

At some point in time, the lure becomes irresistible. They buy a lot. Eventually they build a home. When the conventions of their life "outside" allow, they finally move in and settle permanently. But the outcome was predestined. It was guaranteed the moment they first set foot in Big Canoe.

Many of the permanent residents of Big Canoe are retired, but others are still quite active in the "outside world." Some commute to jobs in Alpharetta or Buckhead. But many are discovering that they can pursue their careers from their homes in Big Canoe, through the internet and other communications links. There are now enough families in Big Canoe with children to fill four school buses each day with students for the schools in Pickens and Dawson counties.

The tie that brings people to Big Canoe is, of course, the land—and the opportunity to use what the land offers for their pleasure and relaxation. Hiking. Golf. Tennis. Boating and canoeing. Fishing.

One outdoor activity that is not permitted in Big Canoe is hunting. Under the covenants of the Property Owners Association, the animals and birds are protected within the 7,600 acres of Big Canoe. Deer, wild turkeys, opossums, and bobcats roam through our backyards and green spaces unmolested. Ducks and geese swim contentedly on the lakes. Woodpeckers, finches, cardinals, and many other species of birds frequent the bird feeders found at most houses.

The human species has adapted nicely to this hospitable environment, building a community that is growing every year, yet perserving the full beauty and charm of the natural environment. The homes blend into the trees and laurel, completely disappearing during the summer.

Big Canoe is a thriving community. Each summer, it absorbs a substantial expansion in numbers, as part-time residents join the full-time residents, and guests arrive for vacations. There are a wide range of recreational activities for the vacationers. But the full-time residents have discovered a deeper reality.

The allure of Big Canoe does not just consist of great golf or never-ending swimming. It is a place that sets each resident free to pursue life as it should be met. It frees each one of us from the conventions and mind sets of daily life in the big city, be it Atlanta or Washington or Chicago.

We don't have to tie ourselves down to a daily commute, or working in a high-rise office. We don't have to subject ourselves to smog and congestion and other irritants. If we want

Spring Lizard Creek in the Nature Valley

17

to have breakfast in May on our decks, we can do so. If we want a full social schedule, we can find it. If we want to study the minerals and rocks of north Georgia, we can do that, too.

For those who worry about life without opera, the theater, or major league sports, downtown Atlanta is only one hour and fifteen minutes away.   Chattanooga, with its aquarium and other attractions, is only a little further to the north. But after a night out, or a day trip to the ball game, there is always a sense of "arrival" as you turn into one of the two gates of Big Canoe.

Those gates provide more than security. They provide a threshold between our two worlds—the world of Big Canoe and the rest of the world. A threshold between the magic of the Enchanted Land and plain old ordinary life.

If you want to do absolutely nothing, there is no better place to do it than Big Canoe. But the corrollary of that sentiment is true as well. Whatever you feel compelled to do, there is no better place to do it than Big Canoe, whether it is write a book, pursue photography, enjoy a round of golf, or compete on the tennis court. It's the ideal place to discover yourself and your talents. It is the perfect place for all kinds of human growth—unless, of course, you want to be a deep sea diver.

A mountain laurel in bloom

18

Sounds of Silence

More than one guest to Big Canoe has been won over by absolutely nothing at all. "I cannot believe how quiet it is up here!" he or she will gush. "Listen to the silence!"

Indeed, listen to the silence. With the exception of the occasional jet cruising overhead at 35,000 feet, there is little to intrude upon Big Canoe's peace and quiet.

As you become acquainted with the silence, it begins to speak to you—silently of course. Immersed in silence, the church bells pealing out the hour at the Big Canoe Chapel gain a new and more powerful resonance. The quiet feet of deer sashaying through the forest bespeak a new level of camaraderie. We are not out of place here. We share something quite important with the deer. Silence.

There are occasions, of course, when our silence is interrupted. A new house is laid out on the lot down the street. Soon, we will hear the bustle of saws and hammers as the walls arise above the foundation. But these are temporary intrusions—necessary interruptions. In a few months, the house will be built, and our life in the woods will be enriched by new neighbors. Silence returns, more glorious than ever.

It is only in silence that we can get to know the true spirit of the place—the very spirit that has enchanted so many people throughout the centuries. Stand on your front porch upon a summer's evening and hear the glorious symphony being performed by Mother Nature: the chirping of the tree frogs, the flapping of moth wings, the crescendoes of crickets. Somehow, it all blends together in a glorious song—an anthem to the night.

It is this kind of silence that lets creative ideas well up in the mind—and lets the calming reassurance of our own inner self heal us from the noisy darts of city living. It lets us rediscover the best within life, the best within ourselves. It is the message of life in Big Canoe.

Hey!

The South has long been recognized as one of the most fertile "valleys" of literary achievement in the whole country. It has produced such greats as William Faulkner, Margaret Mitchell, Sidney Lanier, and James Dickey. This literary richness transfers into the language itself. Sometimes scorned as a "redneck" dialect, "Southern" is actually a distinguished form of speaking, filled with allusions and charm.

Big Canoe attracts folks from all over the country, not just to vacation here, but also to set up residence. Not all of these "transplants," as they are referred to in Georgia, are familiar with Southern idioms. It takes a while to learn.

The first word to learn is "Hey!" It could be translated as "hello," but with proper inflection, it means much more: "Glad to see you. What've you been up to? Is everything going all right?" Southerners are like that. They know how to conserve energy and cram all those ideas into one tidy word. If you meet folks at the post office and they say "Hi" or "Hello," they are not from the South. But if they say "Hey," chances are they have been Southern from the "git go."

Here are some other gems from the Southern lexicon:

Good ole—a term of affection: "good ole truck."

Fixin' to—ready. "I'm fixin' to do that right now."

Much obliged—thank you very much.

Evening—afternoon.

High cotton—prosperity, happiness.

Do go on—you must be joking.

Hard-down good—excellent.

I do declare—a statement of surprise.

Takes a big woman to weigh a ton—stop exaggerating.

Well, shut my mouth!—I am speechless.

Pick up your ears—pay attention.

Church ain't out 'til the fat lady sings—the full version of an oft-misquoted phrase.

Teeing Up

"Golf is a game of misses," says Dave O'Connor, head pro at Big Canoe. "Even the pros seldom hit perfect shots. A tee shot may not stay in the fairway. An approach shot may run 20 feet by the pin. What makes them pros is that they miss their shots much better than the amateur does. In golf, whoever misses the ball the best wins."

The same could be said about Big Canoe golf. With three nine-hole courses traversing the "foothills" of Big Canoe, it may not always deliver perfection—but it seldom misses the mark by very much.

The courses themselves are a delight to play, taking full advantage of the mountainous terrain. It is not at all uncommon to emerge from the woods to stand on a tee box with a view that stretches 50 miles in the distance—as on Cherokee #2—or to find yourself putting out under the inscrutable gaze of the mountains that embrace Big Canoe—as on Creek #9. Other holes wind their way alongside rippling streams, climb or descend the hillsides, or snuggle up to the lapping waves of Lake Sconti.

Dave points out new drainage

Each 9-hole course is named after an Indian tribe that once lived in the area:

Creek, which plays at 3,076 yards from the blue tees, starts with a drive across a finger of Lake Sconti and ends on a green that borders the lake.

Choctaw, playing

Number 1 tee on Choctaw

at 3,230 yards from the blue tees, starts behind the clubhouse parking lot—next to the driving range—and follows a creek out toward Steve Tate Highway. From there, it goes rapidly up-hill, then comes back down to the clubhouse with a devilish, cliff-hanging par 3 over a stream.

Cherokee, which plays 3,169 yards from the blue tees, starts next to the green of Creek #1, and wanders through the high-lands of the Wedgewood neighborhood before making its final

**Dave helps Kate Robertson
with her swing**

descent in one of the most spectacular holes anywhere.

"Our job," Dave continues, is to help everyone who plays these courses to enjoy himself or herself as much as possible. We want our golfers to have as much fun as they can."

A large part of this mission is achieved at the clubhouse, where Dave and his staff maintains a full-service pro shop. When a foursome shows up for a tee time, their golf carts are ready for them, complete with roofs to shade out the sun. In winter, the carts may be equipped with plastic covers, to keep out the worst of the elements.

The pro shop carries a full line of golf equipment, balls, and clothes. "The POA buys the merchandise—everything except the bags and clubs," Dave emphasizes, "and gets twenty percent of what we sell." In a year's time, that is a substantial amount.

Dave came to Big Canoe in 1995 after eight years as head pro at Bay Hill in Orlando, Florida, where he had been hand-picked by Arnold Palmer. His goal is to provide full service. If a golfer needs a club regripped, the staff will do it.

In addition, Dave and his two assistant pros spend much of their time giving lessons, either individually or in classes. Lessons may include work on the driving range, but Dave also teaches "playing lessons"—lessons out on the course.

"If someone hits his drive on Cherokee #1 into the high rough on the right hillside, no amount of practice on the driving range is going to help him hit a decent shot. I have seen player after player try to hit the ball with a fairway wood at a 45° angle in foot-high grass—just because only a wood has the length to reach the green. Of course, he nubs the ball and ends up worse off than he began," Dave explains. "A playing lesson teaches the golfer the fundamentals of playing the ball uphill, downhill, and on the side of hills—very common occurrences on our courses."

This past year, the Creek course has been closed, in order to undergo a thorough overhaul. "It was built 27 years ago, and was pretty well worn out by play," Dave says. "We tore out all of the greens and bunkers and replaced them, so that they all have a new subsurface and improved drainage. The greens were all seeded with bent grass.

"In the process, we also made the course much more playable. Golfers will be surprised by the improvements the first time they play it." On Creek #6, for example, the stream has been relocated so that it runs along the right side of the fairway. This small change makes the hole play entirely differently—and makes it more visually attractive as well.

Big Canoeist Dave Parker (left) buys a golf shirt in the Big Canoe pro shop from Scott Abner

Keeping the Greens

"Mother Nature has a design all her own. We have to respect that design, not try to fight it. We can shape nature, but we cannot force it to act contrary to this design. Ultimately, it is Mother Nature who determines whether the grass grows."

Robbie Womac, head groundskeeper of the Big Canoe golf courses for the past 7 years, is a very wise man. Because he knows how to cooperate with Mother Nature, the greens, fairways, and tees at Big Canoe are almost constantly in near-perfect condition.

"And that is no easy job," he adds. Greenskeepers in Florida can usually head for home by 4 in the afternoon, he says. They plant Bermuda grass, it grows, they cut it, and their work is done. Not so in Big Canoe, which is in a "transition zone" between warm, wet tropical weather and cold, dry temperate weather. Some years, one kind of grass grows well. The next year, the same grass dies— but a different kind flourishes instead.

The terrain is also a challenge for the keeper of the greens. "My first day on the job, I looked at the slopes along the fairways and asked, "How am I ever going to mow those slopes?"

It turned out his crew—he has noth-

Robby Womac on Choctaw #3

ing but praise for his 16 full-time workers—already knew how to mow the slopes. But Womac has learned to let the grasses on slopes grow longer than the normal cut of rough. The longer grass keeps the topsoil from eroding and washing down the hillsides.

"These courses have very little natural topsoil," he explains. "It is important to us to keep the little we have, and not just let it flow into Lake Sconti."

The greens, on the other hand, are mowed every day during the growing season. The tees and fairways are mowed three times a week.

Over the course of a year, Robbie's crew will apply more than 100,000 tons of fertilizer to the three nine-hole courses. They will also apply fungicides and chemicals as needed, to encourage the right kind of growth.

The pace slows a bit in the winter, but Robbie must keep on his toes even then. "The worst damage that can be inflicted by the weather occurs when it turns unusually cold in the winter. Then the chill of the shade created by all of the trees that line the course keep the roots of the grass too wet. They cannot dry out, and may rot."

Greenskeeping is in Robbie's blood. His father is head greenskeeper at Dunwoody Country Club in the north suburbs of Atlanta, and Robbie started doing odd jobs on the golf course when he was 12. At 19, he started his own residential irrigation company, which he ran for 9 years. He then went to college, earned his degree, and returned to Dunwoody as assistant greenskeeper. He left Dunwoody to come to Big Canoe.

He recently became a certified golf superintendent—just one of 1700 people so recognized out of the 20,000 greenskeepers in the United States.

Womac's love for his work and his pride in maintaining the course is immediately evident. It spills over into everything he does. "We deal with a living product. It does not always do what we want it to do, but it is exciting to learn its nature and cooperate with it. That's what we try to do."

Wet & Wild

Nothing defines "summer vacation" more than a sandy beach, a lake, and a whole bunch of kids running around in bathing suits, having fun. Young ones digging in the sand. Older ones playing volleyball. Kids of all ages jumping into the lake and swimming out to a float.

It is a scene that is recreated every single day at Big Canoe from Memorial Day until Labor Day. That is when the swim club is open for business—that is to say, open for vacation.

The swim club provides almost anything aquatic and nautical you might desire. A long stretch of manmade beach, full of sparkling sand, lets you lie on your towel and soak up the sun—if that is your pleasure. The more ambitious can take on the challenge of building sand castles—or a round of volleyball.

Disharoon Lake provides the best of lake swimming, under the supervision of a staff of lifeguards. Next to the lake's dam is a man-made rock slide, which kids of all ages slide down almost constantly.

There is also a brand new swimming pool. After 28 years of valiant service, the old one was too small. (It was being used by an average of 500 people on holiday weekends such as the 4th of July!) So, as part of a new, $5 million amenity package, it was torn out and completely rebuilt during the spring.

Foot-powered paddlewheeler explores the lake

27

Rock slide!

The new pool has a free form shape. The shallow end can be easily entered by young kids who are only able to wade. This leads gradually to a deep end that is 8 feet deep. The whole pool area is set off with picturesque walls and landscaping.

In addition to swimming, the swim club has 15 paddle boats and 13 canoes available for use on Lake Disharoon, except in the areas roped off for swimming.

The swim club lodge provides swimmers with lockers, rest rooms, and a grill that serves hot food and ice-cold drinks. The lodge itself is being partially refurbished as part of the addition of a new fitness center. This project is underway and should be completed by the end of the year.

The completed Fitness Center will include a 5-lane indoor

Kids take to the new pool like a duck to...

Sketch of new pool, swim club, and fitness center

lap pool with an adjacent whirlpool, which will be open year round. The 17,000 square-foot center will also include an exercise room, a racquet ball court, and an aerobics/multi-purpose room. It will run from the swim club lodge to the indoor tennis building.

During the summer, the swim club is run by Allen Bickley, a retired professor at North Georgia College. He oversees a large staff. All lifeguards are trained and certified by the Red Cross and trained in CPR.

The quality of the water in the pool is tested several times every day by the maintenance crew. Those tests are double checked as well by frequent testing by outside agencies.

Courtesy of Debbie Pickett

"We do everything in our powers to maintain the purity of the water in the pool," says Debbie Pickett, administrative assistant for the POA.

Part of the fun to be found at the Swim Club centers around planned activities for children. These range from swimming classes to craft hours.

A little Canoeist paints a ceramic figure in a crafts session

29

Meet Mother Nature

As you drive around Big Canoe, you constantly find yourself on roads such as "Wild Turkey Bluff," "Wildcat Lane," and "Yanoo Trace." You may not have met a yanoo yet—that's Cherokee for bear—but the odds are pretty good that eventually you will.

The mountains of Big Canoe are filled with critters of all kinds—it's part of the charm of the place. The most obvious denizens of the forest are the deer which nimbly roam the hillsides throughout Big Canoe.

A bit less conspicuous, but of similar number, are the wild turkeys which strut throughout the woods like a military unit on parade.

The bear are rarer sights, as they prefer their privacy—and hibernate during the winter—but they can be attracted by the smell of a recent outdoor barbeque. Bears have been known to come up on decks to look for the remains of your last cookout. Among smaller animals, raccoons and possums tend to be regular noctural visitors, although they seem to mind their manners better than some of their counterparts in the suburbs. Foxes and bobcats are less frequently seen, but do live within the bounds of Big Canoe.

One of the best places to observe wildlife is the dam of Lake Petit, where there is almost always a large flock of geese or ducks in residence, as well as otters and beavers.

During the summer, the POA activities committee will sponsor a series of talks by the rangers from Amicalola State Park. Each of the four sessions will educate participants about living with a different aspect of nature: wildflowers, mammals, snakes, and birds of prey.

Sanctuary

Big Canoe is not just a retreat for human beings; it is a sanctuary for animals. The covenants dictate that there will be no hunting of wild life anywhere in the community. In addition, Big Canoe—both the developer and the POA—do everything they can to preserve the natural habitat of our four-footed and winged friends.

It is for this reason that when a tree falls in Big Canoe, it is often left to lie just where it lands—unless it falls across a roadway or a building. Fallen trees provide great homes for all kinds of animals.

Some visitors and residents are tempted every year to feed the animals. "Nature provides plenty of food for them," says Dean Cantrell, head of security for Big Canoe, who advises even against feeding birds.

"I know people like to have birds fly right up to their windows so they can see them, but it's still not a good idea to have birdfeeders. These woods supported animal life for eons before we came. Bears and deer happen to like the sunflower seeds that drop from bird feeders, and may well destroy your garden getting to them."

It's Picnic Time!

Few traditions are more basic to the American lifestyle than a picnic, with hamburgers, hot dogs, bratwurst, potato salad, and chips. Almost every home in Big Canoe has a deck where you can grill out, but that's not the same as picnicking. To picnic, you need wide open spaces where you can toss a frisbee, take a dip, or just relax in the sunshine and take an afternoon snooze—as well as break bread with the ants.

Fortunately, there are numerous options to the picnic-minded resident or visitor to Big Canoe. Picnic tables can be found just about everywhere.

One of the most popular picnic venues is the revamped Swim Club. In addition to a terrific new swimming pool, Big Canoe installed a whole lot of new picnic tables—as well as grills where you can cook up your burgers and brats. Be sure to bring your own charcoal, or pick some up at the General Store close by.

There are also scattered picnic tables at the ball park, the Canoe Lodge, and Nature Valley.

But keep in mind: open fires are not permitted anywhere in Big Canoe. So, if you need fire to cook your food, head for an area with grills.

Barry Pearl dishes up a bratwurst for daughter Danielle

32

Take a Hike

One form of recreation that is indulged in by almost every member of the Big Canoe community—permanent resident, property owner, or vacationer—is hiking. Most of the hikes take place on the 80 miles of roadway that lace through the woods, especially the roads that wind through the neighborhoods, off the "beaten path."

Some of these can be very daunting strolls. One resident regularly walks from his home on Falcon Heights down to Grouse Gap Road, then swings down to the level of Lake Petit as he follows Quail Cove Drive and Osprey Way back to his aerie on top of Wet Mountain. Other folks follow similar regimens in their neighborhoods. It gets the heart pumping.

In fact, researchers say such hiking can be the equivalent of *four* times the exercise of tramping across flat ground.

Of course, you would never find an inveterate hiker such as Henry David Thoreau walking on asphalt. To Thoreau, who wrote an essay on the joys of walking, the best hike is one that strikes out at random across meadows and forests, taking you anywhere and everywhere. For such hikers, there are miles of hiking in every part of Big Canoe, from the just opened trails in McDaniel Meadows to the Lake trail from Indian Rocks park to Lake Petit.

These trails lead you rapidly into Mother Nature's Cathedral of Beauty. They are not meant to be gulped at aerobic speed, but sipped and enjoyed, like fine wine.

Platt nature trail

McDaniel Meadows

The newest addition to Big Canoe's growing assortment of amenities is McDaniel Meadows, a 34-acre park along Wilderness Parkway between Meadowbrook Park and Yanoo Trace, close to the north gate.

Built by the developer, the meadow was officially presented to the Property Owners' Association on September 25, 1999. At that time, it was announced that the meadow would be named in honor of Big Canoe Vice-President Bryant McDaniel.

In citing McDaniel, Big Canoe President Bill Byrne said that much of Big Canoe's enduring beauty is the result of Bryant's stewardship. McDaniel was an early general manager of Big Canoe in the 1970s. He was rehired by Byrne in 1994 to serve as head of development.

Fittingly, McDaniel Meadows exemplifies his commitment to combining outdoor recreation with sensible ecology. A partly paved trail meanders through more than a mile of valley in one of the most picturesque portions of Big Canoe, following a gurgling brook. Plantings of wildflowers are scattered in

Left to right: the gateway to the meadow, Big Canoeists celebrate its opening, and Bryant McDaniel

Ches and June Treadway enjoy an explosion of daisies

patches in the meadows on both sides of the trail. The flowers were planted so as to provide a constant explosion of color and scent from early spring until late fall.

Annuals include cornflowers, pink cosmos, yellow cosmos, rocket larkspur, and gaillardia. Perennials include mountain mint, ox-eyed Daisy, butterfly weed, black-eyed Susan, bachelor's button, Joe-Pye weed, and many more.

The trail itself is an easy grade. Parts are paved, to reduce erosion on slopes and curves. It has become an instant hit with dog owners, who attach their pups to a leash and let the dogs run while they walk, joggers, families; and lots of people taking a refreshing hike.

Although bikes and rollerblades are not allowed in the preserve itself, McDaniel Meadows is a good place to start a "bike hike." A short, paved trail connects the meadow to the soon-to-be-built Wildcat Recreation Center, and from there to the new bike trail across Wildcat Parkway.

In addition to wildflowers, the McDaniel Meadows has also become home for several covey of quail. It is hoped they will put down roots in the dense underbrush along the stream, and become a permanent addition to Big Canoe wildlife.

Indian Rocks

One of the most mystifying corners of Big Canoe is the Indian Rocks park. Scattered—or perhaps carefully arranged—throughout this green area are a dozen or so cairns of rock, each about four feet high and four feet in diameter.

The cairns have been examined, tested, and analyzed by archaeologists, but no definitive answers have been given to the questions: What are they? Why were they built?

Admittedly, this mystery is not quite as profound as those surrounding the pyramids in Egypt or the temples of Macchu Pichu. But there they are—a definite part of the Enchanted Land's magical past.

The rock cairns were built by Indians, probably between 3,000 and 12,000 years ago. They were not used for burial or sacrifice; tests have shown no human remains among the rocks. They were built to stand—and stand they have. Were they used for ceremonies? Or, like Stonehenge, do they have an astronomical significance?

An excellent hiking trail connects the primary cairns. Beginning at a parking area along Woodland Trace, the trail leads up a small hill, where it forks. The left branch loops through the park area; the right branch goes back downhill and takes you to Lake Petit—an endearing trail that runs along one of the streams feeding the lake.

The Nature Valley

One of the most spectacular green areas within Big Canoe is the Nature Valley, a 400-plus-acre tract that is crisscrossed with trails and fascination. The valley is shaped by Disharoon Creek, which meanders between Petit Ridge on the one side and Toland and Disharoon mountains on the other.

Nature Valley can be explored either on foot or by four-wheel drive vehicle. An old logging trail running along Disharoon Creek has been converted into a "Jeep Trail." The Jeep Trail begins just off Buckskull Ridge Road near the Swim Club and wanders north through the valley until exiting on Mountain Mint Drive. From there, Wake Robin will take you over to Petit Ridge Road and back down to the heart of Big Canoe.

It is also possible to enter the Jeep Trail off of Wilderness Parkway. An unmarked dirt road near the creek leads to a small parking area and a tie-in to the trail. It is important to understand, however, that the Jeep Trail is strictly a one-way, north-west bound trail. Do not drive it the wrong way—that is, toward the Swim Club. Also, do not drive it in an ordinary car. There are several fords across the creek, and the road can be muddy after rains. Four-wheel drive is a must.

On foot, the Nature Valley is an endless series of delights. It is easy to see how Big Canoe got the name "the Enchanted

Weaver cabin in the Nature Valley, with running water

The Lower Falls of Disharoon Creek

Land." As you walk along the burbling creek, you begin to adapt from the speeds of human living to the pace of natural time—the pace of trees growing and water etching its way through solid rock.

About a mile and a half from the Swim Club is an old cabin. Although it is called the Disharoon cabin, it was never lived in by the Disharoon family. It was part of a cabin lived in by Pete Weaver, brought from outside Big Canoe and set on the site of the Disharoon homestead.

From the cabin, you can take the "Cabin Loop Trail," then follow the hiking trail to the Lower Falls—and eventually to the Upper Falls.

One of several fords on the Jeep Trail

Loop the Lake

There you are: sunning yourself on the beach at Lake Disharoon, and an impulse suddenly comes to you to get some exercise. You could just go for a swim, of course, but there is another option as well. Loop the lake!

"Loop the Lake" is the name of the trail that begins at the swim club and follows, more or less, the contour of Lake Disharoon. From the swim club, the path heads over to the Jeep Trail, then turns back along the lake's edge. It meets with the beginning of the Nature Valley trail at its nethermost point, then swings back and heads along the west side of Disahroon, over the dam, and up to the swim club again. The whole trail is about two miles long—a nice 45-minute interlude on a sunny day.

Of course, if you are not swimming, you can enter the trail at either its connection with the Jeep Trail or the start of the Nature Valley trail, just off Wilderness Parkway (where you can park the car).

For those who like their hikes to be easy saunters, this trail is ideal. If you start at Wilderness Parkway, you will arrive at the swim club halfway through your trek. After an hour or so relaxing at the grill, you can then resume your hike, fully refreshed and ready for whatever adventures lie ahead!

Hiking Etiquette

There are 15 miles of enjoyable hiking trails within Big Canoe. As you hike, please follow these rules:

1. Stay on the path.
2. Do not litter.
3. Do not pick wildflowers—leave them to be enjoyed by the people just behind you on the trail.
4. Do not carve initials in trees or deface rocks.
5. Leave your radio at home.

Robert Platt Trail

For Big Canoeists looking for a short hike, one of the most interesting trails is the Robert Platt Memorial Trail, linking the Robert Platt Botanical Gardens with Wilderness Parkway, just south of the covered bridge.

Owned and maintained by the Big Canoe Chapel, this trail is best approached by driving out of the main gate, turning left on Steve Tate Highway, and then immediately turning left into the driveway between two stone columns. This leads you into a tract of ground that was given by the developer to the Chapel

for its use. So far, this use consists of the Robert Platt Botanical Gardens, the cemetery, and the ampitheatre, now under construction.

The Botanical Gardens are a work in progress. An old cabin has been moved to the spot to serve as an anchor for the various specimens of native flowers and trees planted in the area.

The trail starts at the cabin and follows the stream that eventually crosses Wilderness Parkway at the covered bridge. It is a delightful walk through laurel thickets and the woods. If you have sharp eyes and a lot of imagination, you may even be able to spot some rusted reminders of years and years ago, when bootleggers took advantage of the water power flowing through the stream to distil whiskey for their customers. The still was destroyed by "revenooers" years ago, and most of its remains have now vanished.

Tennis Anyone?

Howard Hunt had a fairly predictable life just a few years ago. As a professional tennis player, he spent about half the year in the United States, playing in tournaments and making personal appearances. He would then head to Europe to play for a few months, and would winter in his native Australia.

He had never even heard of Big Canoe.

But a few years ago, while in his native Perth, he met Lyn, who became his wife. He brought Lyn to the United States where he had an offer for a position as a tennis pro. He took it, but the property was sold for other development. Lyn and Howard were about to head for Australia when Howard learned about a quaint mountain community in north Georgia that was looking for an accomplished tennis pro. They drove up to look the place over, fell in love with it, and took the job.

They set up home in a condo overlooking Lake Sconti, but lost it a year ago to a fire. They now live in a home in Shetland Trace, and have come to expect the unpredictable.

In the meantime, they have re-energized the Big Canoe tennis program. In the two years since they arrived, tennis play has increased 300 percent.

Howard teaching
Big Canoeist Peg Ewing

They make a good team. Howard, a former junior champion in Australia who has been ranked as one of the top 25 tennis professionals in the world, handles the teaching. Lyn, who had been in an office environment before marrying Howard, has put her skills to work running the pro shop.

"At one time, the tennis program in Big Canoe was aimed at people who already played tennis," Howard explains. "That's not enough—we want to encourage anyone who might enjoy tennis to come play."

"We want people to realize how much fun tennis can be," adds Lyn.

Toward this end, Howard has greatly expanded the teaching programs. He is especially proud of the classes he holds for ladies.

"Many of these women have never played tennis before," he says. "But now there kids are at college or working and they have moved to Big Canoe and have time on their hands. They are coming to the courts and hitting balls for an hour every Wednesday, and they are really enjoying it."

"We are focusing now on encouraging couples to play tennis together—and with other couples," Lyn adds. For Easter weekend, they scheduled a tennis mixer and cookout. They asked the participants to show up in Easter bonnets and hats, giving prizes for best entries. After the tennis, they held a cookout.

"Tennis is a social sport," Lyn continues. "We are trying to help the residents and guests of Big Canoe discover that."

The tennis facilities are built around the historic Wolfscratch school building used by the Tate Mountain School—a building built 85 years ago. The original chestnut panelling on the walls still graces the interior, where the pro shop is.

Outside is a deck where they hold cookouts, and beyond are the courts—four hydro soft courts and four hard courts. Half are lighted for night play. Across the street are two indoor courts, used when weather prohibits the use of outdoor courts.

As with the golf shop, the tennis shop is well stocked with all of the clothes, equipment, and accessories needed to enjoy the

Tennis towel

game of tennis. Need a racquet restrung? Howard and Lyn can do it for you. Have a kid who would love to learn to play tennis? Howard has a junior program that will have him or her swinging in no time.

Lyn restrings a racquet

"You'd be surprised how popular our junior programs are," Howard says, "and not just in summer. There are more and more families coming to Big Canoe while still raising their children. They go to school during the day, then come over here to play tennis after the school bus drops them off."

Howard and Lyn take the attitude that "there is no such thing as a problem—just new opportunities for continuous improvement. " It's the attitude of a champion—and a champion program.

43

The Lakes

"There is nothing as beautiful as gliding along on Lake Petit, looking up at the mountains towering overhead," says Sally Williams, co-chair with husband John of the Lakes Committee.

Eighty-five years ago, none of the four lakes of Big Canoe existed. Sconti was the heart of the agricultural experiments of the Tate Educational Foundation. A large concrete silo towered over fields. But in the Twenties, Sam Tate decided to abandon his experimental farms, and built the dam creating Lake Sconti—leaving the silo to tower above the water.

When Tom Cousins planned Big Canoe, he realized the importance of lakes—for beauty, fishing, boating, swimming, and sales appeal. Finding the water was no problem—streams abound in Big Canoe. But it was necessary to add dams. Two dams were built on Disharoon and Petit creeks, creating two more majestic lakes: Lake Disharoon and Lake Petit.

Later, during construction of the Cherokee golf course, a fourth lake was built.

Lake Sconti, named after a Cherokee chief who lived in the region around 1800, became the central focus of Big Canoe. Lake Sconti—with the silo now removed—makes the perfect backdrop for golfing—the Creek course encircles it. It is also

An entry in the annual decorated boat contest

the ideal setting for the Lake Sconti restaurant and clubhouse. Looking out the windows of the restaurant, it is possible to see the mountains that encircle Big Canoe.

Lake Disharoon, named for the Disharoon clan, is the home of the Swim Club. Other than the canoes and paddlewheelers that are part of the Swim Club, boating is not permitted.

The primary venue for boating, canoeing, and fishing is the largest of the three lakes—Lake Petit, named not for its size but for one of the families that used to live along Petit Creek.

Hundreds of Big Canoe families own boats or canoes and moor them on Lake Petit, either at the marina or at the boat launch at the far end of the lake. The marina is located along Wilderness Parkway, just beyond the dam. The boat ramp is located off Quail Cove Drive, near Osprey Drive. Its storage area has recently been revamped and expanded, to accommodate the growing number of private boats at Big Canoe.

Most of the craft are pontoon boats, row boats, or canoes, but there are a few kayaks and one rowing scull in the group. No gasoline engines are allowed, although small electric motors may be used.

Docking boats at Lake Petit requires a permit.

Gone Fishin'

Izaak Walton, in his book on fishing, *The Compleat Angler,* put it thus: "As no man is born an artist, so no man is born an angler." Fishing is a pursuit that requires interest, skill, the time to pursue it—and a lake or stream full of fish.

Big Canoe provides the lakes, and has attracted hundreds of fisher people to fish them.

The best fishing is in Lake Petit, which extends to depths as great as 98 feet. This makes it somewhat like an Alpine lake; the water at the bottom stays very cold.

The primary fish in Petit are rainbow trout. The lakes and fishing committee of the POA stock the lake on a regular basis. Some bass also live in the lake, although they are not stocked.

Some people fish from the dam or the shore around the lake; some fish from canoes. Others troll slowly in boats with electric motors. Each has his or her own secrets for catching the big ones—and each has his or her own share of fish stories to tell friends and family.

Fishing is not limited to Petit, although it is the only lake that is stocked. As long as you have the necessary POA fishing

The catch that shows that clinics work!

permit (annual or daily), you can fish in Sconti as well. Fishing is also permitted in certain areas of Lake Disharoon, away from the swimming.

A 10-pound bass was recently caught by a golf pro fishing in Lake Sconti. The largest fish on record is a 13 1/2-pound bass pulled out of Lake Petit.

Fishing is actively supported in Big Canoe. The lakes and fishing committee holds fishing clinics and tournaments throughout the year. The clinics are held for the young and adults alike, and cover all the basics of fishing in detail. Two or three bass tournaments are held each year.

Fishing opportunities at Big Canoe will expand even further as the Wildcat neighborhood is developed. Several excellent trout streams run through the area and will be preserved as interconnected recreation areas.

Proceeds from the annual and daily fishing permits are used to keep the lake well stocked.

No, this is not the work of a frustrated angler. The wind flipped this moored boat on its top a few years ago.

Lake Sconti Restaurant

"We serve about 900 meals every week," says POA Food Services Manager Jonathan Cheatham. "If we cater special functions, it can be even more than that. We know we are important to the community—and are determined to meet its needs."

Jonathan, who signed on to head the food services at Big Canoe in the fall of 1999, is dedicated to providing good food services. The problem, he says—and he quickly adds that it is also the opportunity—is that the role of Lake Sconti Restaurant is changing as the size of Big Canoe expands.

"Some people expect us to be their clubhouse, a casual place where they can order a steak after 18 holes of golf—or where a bridge party of 40 ladies can have lunch along with cards. But others would prefer that we be a four-star restaurant, offering impeccable service as well as exquisite food. We are trying to define the needs of the community, so that we can meet them."

Friday night at Sconti

In addition to the Sconti, which serves breakfast, lunch, dinner, and brunch on different days through out the week, food services runs Duffer's at the golf course—and provides catering as needed.

The Sconti serves beer and wine, but does not have a license to serve spirits. Application has been made for such a license, but may require time.

Still, dining at the

Sconti can be a tonic for the spirit just about any time of the year. The view across Lake Sconti toward the mountains is always uplifting—a marvelous setting.

The Sconti kicked off its new season of buffet dinners recently with great success. On Friday nights, they put on a seafood buffet for $17.95, with salmon, shrimp, crawfish, several types of whitefish, hush puppies, vege-

Chef Howard Newton dishing up

tables, and an excellent salad bar. Each Saturday night, they offer a prime rib buffet for $12.95.

The restaurant also serves dinner every Wednesday evening, the POA's community dinner. The menu is posted each week by the POA on channel 12 and the web site; reservations are required.

In addition, a lunch buffet is served every weekday; it is also possible to order a la carte. Jonathan says that he and Chef

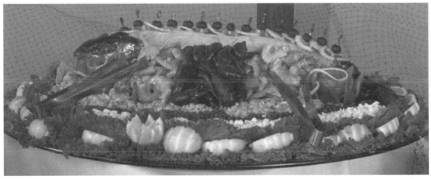

Piece d' resistance: salmon with shrimp and crawfish

49

Hostess Amy Pool hands change to waiter Josh Early;
8-year resident Gary Lawson helps himself to the buffet

Howard Newton have been working on a new menu for lunch, which should debut soon.

The Sconti is also open for breakfast from 7 to 10 on both Saturday and Sunday, and for brunch on Sunday from 11 to 3.

"The Sconti belongs to the community," Jonathan adds. "We are here to serve its needs."

Jonathan Cheatham surveys the Sconti bar

The General Store

Need to gas up the car? Buy a loaf of bread? Looking for night crawlers—or fishing gear—to snag a fish or two in Lake Petit?

The place to go is the Wolfscratch Village General Store, founded in the late 70's and still serving the needs of a growing community.

Currently run by Ann French, the General Store is one of the primary gathering places for Big Canoe residents—although not usually all at once! It is a place to come for a copy of the Sunday newspaper, select a bottle of fine wine, stock up on food, buy a Big Canoe license plate for the front of the car, or pick up emergency aspirin.

"We have three markets we serve," says Ann: "the permanent community, vacationers, and construction workers.

"Residents tend to stop by for gas or to buy snacks and food. Some are quite regular, stopping in once or even twice a day. Vacationers will pick up food, but also are looking for things

Cashier Christina Travis hands resident Fred Shaw his change

like our Big Canoe T-shirts and souvenirs. Construction workers visit us to buy lunch and soft drinks. With 100 or more homes being built each year now, the workers are a big source of sales to us."

All of the sandwiches sold at the store are made by hand in an upstairs kitchen every day.

Originally, the General Store also housed the post office—then a contract operation, meaning the residents could buy stamps and mail packages. That changed, however, when the post office was moved to its present location.

At present, the upstairs houses the store's collection of video tapes, which can be rented for the night, plus antique items for sale. There are also tables where lunch customers can sit and relax while they eat their sandwiches, and a lending library of donated books, which can be borrowed under the honor system.

The store is open every day from 8 in the morning until 8 at night. During the peak summer months, from Memorial Day to Labor Day, Ann's staff grows as large as 6 part-timers.

The busiest weekend of the year? July 4th. "We can easily have 20 customers in the store at once over that weekend."

"We try to serve the community," Ann says. "We do not have resort-style prices. We are not interested in gouging anyone."

The store is located in Wolfscratch Village, the first right turn after entering the village from Wolfscratch Road.

Our Indian Heritage

Human beings have lived in the north Georgia mountains for at least 17,000 years. Needless to say, the information we have today about the original inhabitants—or even if they were the original inhabitants—is sketchy and incomplete.

According to current scientific thinking, Paleo Indians inhabited this region about 15000 BC. They were a nomadic culture, dependent largely on hunting, fishing, and gathering for their food supply. Their pottery and tools were very primitive, but they did use open pit firing to make their earthenware.

Somewhere around 8000 BC, these people were replaced by what is called the Archaic Indians. Their civilization resembled the Paleos in many ways, but they were probably more sophisticated in their use of tools and the nature of their pottery.

The Woodland tribes began to inhabit the region in 5000 BC. These were the first Indians to build permanent villages and cultivate the land.

The Mississippian Indians occupied the region from about 400 AD to 1200 AD. Spanning a vast area from Wisconsin to Georgia to Mississippi to the Great Plains, these tribes traded with each other, were accomplished craftsmen, and held sophisticated religious beliefs. In their myth of creation, for example, the earth was formed when the Great Buzzard, flying over the earth, began flapping his wings. Each flap formed a mountain or a valley, or created an ocean or a river. By the time he flew away, the earth—Turtle Island—had been shaped and populated.

The Mississippians in Georgia were mound builders—but their mounds were used for city planning, instead of protection or burial. The highest mound was reserved for the chief. Lower mounds were occupied by lesser leaders. In between, on flat land, was the ceremonial plaza which was the heart of village life.

Excellent examples of these mounds still survive today at the Etowah Indian Mounds State Historic Site, five miles from exit 12A on I-75 near Cartersville. The highest mound reaches a height of 63 feet.

The mound building Indians were followed by the Historic Tribes, the Creeks and Cherokees. The Creeks were the dominant tribe in Georgia until the pressure of westward-moving settlers forced the Cherokees into north Georgia.

Sequoyah, a Cherokee chief

The Creek Confederacy—now the Creek Nation—migrated to the Southeast from the Southwest. They lived in villages built around a central plaza. In the middle of the plaza was a round building used for council meetings. Family homes, made of poles and mud, surrounded the plaza. Creeks did not live in teepees.

The Cherokees are descendants of the Iroqouis. The name means "the Principal People." Like the Creeks, they were an agrarian tribe that lived in log huts in villages. By 1650, the Cherokees controlled an area of southern Appalachia exceeding 40,000 square miles. They had a population estimated at 22,500.

As European settlers gained more and more of a foothold in the area, the Cherokees tried hard to adapt to the new ways. They created an alphabet which let them transfer spoken Cherokee into written form. They set up a capital in New Echota—thirty miles west of Big Canoe—and issued a regular newspaper in Cherokee. Many of them adopted Christianity. They dressed in European clothes and adopted many European customs. In fact, they were the second largest ethnic group of slave owners in the United States!

The New Echota State Historic Site is located just north of the intersection of Highway 53—the road running through Marble Hill and Jasper—and I-75, near Calhoun. It is open Tuesday through Sundays. Admission is charged.

Funk Heritage Center

Want to learn more about the Indian tribes that once lived and hunted in Big Canoe? Or the life of the early settlers who came after?

One of the best places to go to learn the story of north Georgia's past is the Funk Heritage Center, a brand new

The Funk Center

complex being developed at Reinhardt College in Waleska.

The Funk center consists of three parts: the Bennett History Museum, a replica of a pioneer settlement, and a nature trail.

The museum is built in the style of a Cherokee long house, where several families would live together. The great hall in the center of the museum is filled with artifacts from the days of the Indians as well as pioneer times. One of the most interesting specimens is an authentic dugout canoe. In all, some 5,000 Indian artifacts have been donated to the exhibit by various residents of Cherokee County.

A short movie traces the appearance and disappearance of various Indian tribes throughout the years, and recounts aspects of Indian legend and lore. In a separate gallery, the village life of each stage of Indian develop-

A full size animated figure speaks of the past

ment is depicted in a sequence of excellent dioramas. A third gallery contains an impressive display of contemporary Indian art, sculpture, and crafts.

Temporary exhibits are presented in yet another room. This spring, a very convincing animated figure of a living native American, Amy Walker, has been telling the story of her search for the roots of the spiritual traditions of her people, the Cherokee nation.

The museum also houses a splendid exhibit of tools used by

End view of dugout canoe

hand craftsmen of all kinds of trade during the early days of the country, up to the 20th century. The collection was donated to the museum by Alan Sellars, a resident of Cobb County. There are tools of carpenters, sawyers, surveyors, artists, printers, prospectors—more than 10,000 tools in all, each kind dramatically displayed on individual panels.

Chiquita Berry employs an apple corer

On leaving the museum, a trail leads toward the Appalachian Settler's Village, a reconstruction of an early north Georgia village and farmstead. Pioneer log cabins have been located and transported to this site, where they are being restored and refurbished with tools and furniture from the early days. The goal is to recreate an authentic replica of an early settlement, com-

Printing Tools

plete with farm animals, a pond, and workshops, such as a blacksmith's shop.

Still in the works is a "discovery trail," a three-quarter mile path which will lead visitors on a tour of wilderness living. Part of the trail already exists, pointing out trees and other vegetation used by Indians and the early settlers in their daily lives.

"The goal is to create the experience of living history," says Chiquita Berry, a master gardener who volunteers at the museum and was our guide into the past.

The Funk Center opened in November of 1999. Some of the exhbits are still in development. But it is a fascinating place to visit and learn more about life 200 years ago.

To get there, take Highway 53 west to where it turns right to Jasper. Keep going straight on Route 108, which will take you into Waleska. Turn right into the Reinhardt College campus, then right again toward the Funk Center. Admission is $5 for adults.

Volunteer Frank Stone works with a planer

The Trail of Tears

The Cherokees made one very serious error. During the Revolutionary War and again in the War of 1812, they sided with the British against the Americans. The major campaigns launched by the Cherokees against American forces ended in disaster and humiliation for the Cherokees. They lost a lot of their land as a result and were forced to consolidate their nation in western North Carolina and northern Georgia.

Unfortunately for the Cherokees, gold was discovered in north Georgia in 1828. The epicenter of the Georgia gold rush was in Dahlonega, just twenty miles from Big Canoe. The words "gold mine road" still appear in many area street names today.

The federal government, remembering the role the Cherokees had played in the war, negotiated a treaty to purchase all of the Cherokee lands east of the Mississippi for $5 million. The Cherokees were granted new lands in Oklahoma.

The treaty was not popular with the majority of the tribe, however. At this time, the population of Cherokees in north Georgia was about 20,000. A great many of them refused to leave their lands voluntarily, even though the $5 million had been accepted by the nation.

In 1838, about 18,000 Cherokees were rounded up by federal troups and forced to resettle in Oklahoma. Three thousand more managed to elude the troops, and hid out in the mountains of north Georgia. It was a rough trip to Oklahoma—the trail of tears. Four thousand of the 18,000 Cherokees died of disease and the rigors of the wintry journey. In addition, disgruntled Cherokees exacted deadly reprisals on fellow tribe members who had accepted the treaty.

Still, the Cherokee nation was successful in re-establishing its culture in Oklahoma. And the 3,000 who remained in Georgia came out of hiding and resumed their lives. Today, they number 20,000—the number who lived here before the "trail of tears."

The First Goldrush

In Cherokee, the word for "gold" is "Tahlonega." When the first white man heard the word, he did not wait around long enough to master the pronunciation. He picked up his shovel and headed for Dahlonega, the site of the first big gold rush in America—20 years before Sutter's Creek, 70 years before Alaska. And, if the truth be known, there is still gold in the mountains of North Georgia.

How much gold was mined out of the mountains? Enough to warrant building a U.S. mint in Dahlonega. Enough to make the mint one of the first federal properties seized by the Confederacy during the civil war. Enough to make Dahlonega a legit boom town until the fever spread elsewhere.

Now Dahlonega is just a charming tourist town, and the home of the North Georgia College. A courthouse from the days of prosperity stills stands in the central plaza downtown. It has been converted into a fascinating museum about the Dahlonega gold rush and how the precious yellow metal was extracted from the unyielding Appalachian mountains.

Commercial mining in the area died out rapidly after the end of the Civil War, even though a fair amount of gold deposits still remain. If you want to try your hand at panning for gold, several old mines that now cater to tourists will be glad to rent you a pan and show you how to go about working it. The odds of discovering a speck or two of gold are a lot better than winning the lottery—and won't cost much more. Put enough of those specks together, and you too can be a prospector who struck it big in Georgia.

There is definitely still enough gold in north Georgia to refinish the dome of the Georgia state capitol with new gold leaf every now and then.

Is there gold in Big Canoe? Most likely. But it is not highly probable that any of it is still in the ground, undiscovered. It is more likely to be in family safes—as Kruggerands or jewelry.

Of Mountains and Men

The mountains have been here for millions of years. The men arrived only recently, by comparison. But oddly enough, the mountains are named after the men, not the other way around. It would seem that men, who are very mortal, would want to be named after mountains, which are not. But human customs are often strange.

There are eight mountains within the confines of Big Canoe. Seven are on the west side of Steve Tate Highway; Potts Mountain is on the east side, and has yet to be developed. Most of the mountains are named after the people who sold their property to Sam Tate when he was acquiring the land for the Tate Mountain School, around 1900. They are:

Cox Mountain—Tobe and Martha Cox raised a family of 11 children—three more died in childbirth—in a small cabin at the base of Cox Mountain. They lived on the land from 1884, when they first married, until they sold it to Tate.

Disharoon Mountain—Isaac and Mary Disharoon owned hundreds of acres in the Nature Valley area. They lived in a commodious log home—much larger than the cabin that now occupies the spot of their homestead.

Toland Mountain—According to legend, as reported in Charlene Terrell's book, *Wolfscratch Wilderness,* Toland was a stranger who died on this mountain many years ago.

The Big Canoe skyline from the Sconti clubhouse

Sanderlin Mountain—John and Mary Sanderlin lived on the slope of Sanderlin Mountain in the 1850's, before John enlisted in the Confederate Army and was killed in the war. Although they only lived there a short while, their appellation has endured. Interestingly, the mountain had been called Sconti Mountain before the Sanderlins moved there.

Wet Mountain—Apparently, no one of importance lived here prior to Sam Tate buying up all of the land, so it is just called Wet Mountain—perhaps in tribute to the fine old art of moonshining, which was widely practiced in this area.

McElroy Mountain—John and Delilah McElroy moved into the area of the McDaniel Meadows in 1860, built a home—the twin chimneys and foundation can still be found on the north side of the meadows—and settled down to raise a family and farm. Their property embraced McElroy Mountain to the northwest.

Little McElroy Mountain—This smaller peak was the other bookend to the McElroy family property.

Across Steve Tate Highway, **Potts Mountain** acquired its name from the Potts family, which lived there from the days of the Dahlonega gold rush.

The names of Big Canoe's lakes also preserve its past. **Lake Sconti** is named after a Cherokee chieftain who lived on the Wolfscratch land. **Lake Petit** is named for the family of Dave Petit, who farmed the cove that is now Big Canoe's largest lake.

Potts Mountain

61

A Tragedy in 3 Acts

If William Shakespeare were alive today, he might consider the story of the Tate family of Georgia worthy of retelling as a tragedy—a tragedy without murder, but with plenty of hubris.

The play begins in the 1830's, when Samuel Tate bought from Ambrose Harnage a tavern and surrounding land on the Old Federal Road. He continued to run the inn, but soon discovered a major vein of marble on the property—a vein that ran for several miles. Samuel—and his son Stephen after him—developed the marble by leasing the lands to mining companies, and then acquiring more lands with marble deposits. In this way, the family became quite wealthy.

Stephen had a son whom he named Samuel, after his father. Samuel the younger turned out to be something of a wastrel, and soon became an alcoholic. But he finally conquered his addiction and opened a general store.

In 1884, the Georgia Marble Company was organized to oversee the mining operations. In 1905, Sam sold his general store and bought a controlling share in Georgia Marble.

Act Two: In 1909, some of the leases to the mining companies expired, so Sam began an ambitious campaign to buy up all of the mining operations and deposits in north Georgia, and run them under the umbrella of the Georgia Marble Company. In doing so, he sowed the seeds of eventual destruction, as he carelessly intermingled family assets with company assets.

Once Tate—now known as Colonel Sam—had cornered the market on marble mining, he turned his attention to buying up land in the region. He had a project in mind: he wanted to build a school in the mountains for the hardscrabble folks who lived there and teach them experimental approaches to agriculture. Of course, in order to reach his goal, he displaced many of the families he was driven to help.

In the Roaring Twenties, Sam built the lavish marble palace that still stands in Tate, Georgia, and lived there with his brother Luke and his sister Flora. He also inaugurated a resort community called Tate Mountain Community just to the north of Highway 136. As the experimental farm at the mountain school became impractical, Sam built Lake Sconti and converted the property—basically the lands that became Big Canoe—to a second home. Sam never married, although he left behind plenty of children throughout the mountains.

Act Three. Tragedy beset the Tate family when Luke Tate, son of Sam's brother Walt and heir apparent at Georgia Marble to Sam, died when his speedboat hit the silo in Lake Sconti. As the Depression set in, the ability of Georgia Marble to continue making a profit dropped each year. In 1934, Sam had to arrange bank financing to keep Georgia Marble operating. As the cash flow shrank, relatives began to sue Sam for mismanaging his father's estate.

Before he died in 1938, Sam deeded the mountain school property to his nephew Steve. Relatives who had sued were cut out of his will entirely. When they discovered that Sam had also deeded thousands of acres to Steve, a major war broke out among family members.

Steve spent most of the last 20 years of his life fighting to save his land. In 1941, Sam's estate was declared insolvent; its creditors in turn also questioned the validity of Sam's land transfer to Steve. Eventually, Steve agreed to pay $10,000 to the estate to get clear title to the property, where he and his wife Lucille were now living.

It was not long before the Internal Revenue Service began to dig into the transactions of Georgia Marble—especially the commingling of family and corporate assets, inaugurated by Sam Tate and imitated by Steve Tate. Steve also made the error of failing to file income taxes in 1944. In the face of the claims against him, Steve became an alcoholic. In 1958, he died—perhaps by his own hand, perhaps by the bottle. Shortly thereafter, his home burned down, leaving only two chimneys.

Lucille had to sell Wolfscratch to settle Steve's affairs. Thus ends the Tate drama—and sets the stage for Big Canoe.

Tate Mountain School

Colonel Sam Tate was a man with a large ego and a some-what narrower vision. He tried very hard to create his own personal empire in the northwoods of Georgia—and largely succeeded during his lifetime. But the empire was not put together very well, and it fell apart once he died. He was unable to insure the success of the crown prince, nephew Steve.

It is fairly clear that he viewed the families that lived in north Georgia with him as his personal vassals. The men all worked for him at Georgia Marble Company at one time or another, and often in other enterprises as well. In his zeal to buy up as much property as possible in north Georgia, he entered into real estate dealings with almost every family in Pickens County.

In medieval times, the vassals did the bidding of their lord, but the lord likewise had a responsibility to the vassals—to protect them, feed them, and educate them. During the Depression, Colonel Sam did his best to create work for the unemployed in the area, until his own resources began to run out. It was characteristic of the man. Thirty years earlier, he had embarked on a scheme to educate the people of the region—a scheme that made Big Canoe possible.

It was around the turn of the century that Sam first conceived of the idea of establishing an experimental mountain farm and school in the area known as Wolfscratch—an old Indian hunting ground that straddled the line between Pickens and Dawson counties, near the center of what is now Big Canoe. Toward that end, he began patiently buying up property in the area.

When he had acquired sufficient land, he hired a man named Joseph Riis to start the experimental farm. Joseph was the son of a well-known author, Jacob Riis, and had been a forest ranger in the Grand Tetons. With the help of a crew of mountain men, Riis built a huge concrete silo in the middle of what is now Lake Sconti. At that time, it was the center of the Tate farm.

Barns were also built, and a spacious home that was intended to house Riis and his family, plus any schoolteachers working at the mountain school. It burned down in 1958 (when it was the home of Lucille Tate), but its two chimneys remain in the heart of Big Canoe as testimony to a bold vision.

The two-room mountain school was built by the volunteer efforts of the men in the surrounding area. The men who built it insisted on naming it "Wolfscratch School," even though Sam Tate disliked the Indian name and did not want to use it.

The school educated mountain children from 1917 to 1929. A total of five teachers were employed at various times during the five years, and 45 children received their education in the school. The largest enrollment at the school in any one year was 20 students.

The farm was operated from 1915 to about 1925. Sam Tate tried to cultivate everything from grain to cattle. One of his greater follies was an attempt to raise a herd of deer. The deer kept getting off the property and causing damage to the farms of Tate's neighbors. Finally, he turned them loose.

Once the vision of an experimental farm had failed, Tate decided to convert the Wolfscratch property into a private recreational preserve. He planned and built the dam which created Lake Sconti. Unfortunately, the water level was not high enough to cover up the concrete silo, which was left standing in spite of being in the middle of the lake. Tate commissioned estimates to remove the silo, but decided he would rather look at the silo than pay that much money.

Tate changed his mind after his nephew Luke crashed a speedboat into the silo and died. The silo was dismantled.

The property that Tom Cousins bought in order to create Big Canoe was essentially the property that Sam Tate had put together in order to create his farm and mountain school. The schoolhouse is now the tennis pro shop. An original barn, converted to a home by Lucille Tate after the Riis home burned, today houses the headquarters of the POA.

In a way, Sam's vision still survives—as Big Canoe.

The Countryside Café

It may have seemed a rash step for a young married couple to take. But nine years ago, John and Cindy Lupi took the gamble of their lives anyway. They bought a struggling restaurant serving Southern cuisine just outside the north gate of Big Canoe, in the heart of the north Georgia mountains, in the hopes of turning it into a culinary showcase.

Nine years later, they are succeeding beyond their dreams. Under their loving direction, The Countryside Café has become a favorite dining spot not just for folks in Big Canoe, but also as far away as Dunwoody, Alpharetta, Canton, and Ellijay.

The Lupis re-earn their reputation with every lunch and dinner they serve. Since taking over the restaurant, they have redecorated the inside, expanded the dining area, totally replaced the kitchen equipment, and introduced a lively, contemporary cuisine. They have also multiplied their business five-fold.

Jill & Henry Morgan celebrate their anniversary

John checks on the rising of the bread

In fact, they introduce a new menu every two months—by design. Some of the items remain constant—there is always fresh rainbow trout on the menu, and almost always beef tenderloin—but even then, the way in which the dishes are sauced changes.

"We believe that if the items were to remain the same, we might become complacent in preparing them. I want everyone working in the kitchen to be own their toes—challenged by what we serve," John Lupi explains. "So we come up with a new menu every two months."

As chef, John says he follows current trends, but is not limited by them. "Our primary aim in selecting the menu is to try to use local ingredients whenever possible." He develops all of the recipes for the entreés himself.

Choosing the right ingredients is just the beginning of the process, though. Every dish that is served is created entirely in the Countryside kitchen—from every roll of bread to every serving of the desserts that demand to be eaten.

Perfection does not come cheap, of course. A bowl of the Lobster Bisque costs $7.95. But it is well worth the price. It is hard to imagine a more glorious soup, spoonful for spoonful. There is also a "soup of the day" which varies from menu to menu, and is considerably less expensive.

In addition to soups, each menu offers several appetizers and salad

Rosie prepares tonight's Tiramisu

Cindy selects a Champy Pere '96

courses, a la carte. It is often possible to make an exciting meal out of a soup, a salad, and an appetizer.

All entrees are served with a potato dish and vegetable designed to match the entrée perfectly. The filet, exquisitely cooked and sauced, came with a delightful dish of Potato Dauphinoise—a pudding of white and sweet potatoes—as well as asparagus. The salmon was sauced with dill and cucumber, accompanied by braided strands of whipped potatoes and asparagus. The placement of the food on the plates matched the taste in style and appeal.

It would be sacrilege, however, to dine at the Countryside without having dessert. The signature dessert, Raspberry White Chocolate Cheesecake, has been on the menu since the restaurant opened, and is highly popular. A serving of Tiramisu, freshly assembled an hour before by Rosie Wentworth, was also superb! There is always a tempting selection.

The wine list is well thought out; in general, you can rely on any wine in their cabinet to be a pleasure.

Cindi and John hint that their days of expansion are not over. Plans are afoot to open a small gourmet shop in the lobby of the restaurant by the end of the year, offering foods prepared in the restaurant for carry out, as well as gifts and other items.

The Countryside Café is an enchanting place to dine.

John slices the potatoes Dauphinoise into servings

Moonshine Nights

Whiskey, you're the devil,
You're leadin' me astray,
O'er the hills and mountains
Unto Americay...

Probably to the hills of north Georgia, where illegal boot-legging was a flourishing, albeit clandestine, industry from the 1870's until the 1940's.

Prior to the income tax, liquor taxes were one of the primary sources of income for the federal government. Mountain folk did not want to pay these taxes, and so a black market arose for the manufacture and sale of illegal booze. All a bootlegger needed was a lot of bravado, the materials, the equipment, and a nice, secluded spot along a rapidly running mountain stream—preferably not on his own property! It had to be private enough that the smoke from the fire would not be visible to "revenooers."

Thousands of such stills sprung up in the north Georgia mountains. Rusty remnants of some of them can still be found within the confines of Big Canoe, which was a popular spot for the whisky men. But the memory of moonshine still lives on, most notably on April 15th of every year. For the modern day Internal Revenue Service, which now breaks up the calm and peaceful lives of taxpayers, was originally the department of government that smashed the stills of bootleggers.

Colonel Sam Tate, incidentally, disliked the presence of boot-legging in the region intensely. Although an alcoholic in his early adulthood, he gave up drinking after the death of his mother, and became an ardent opponent of the illegal trade.

Fifty years later, his nephew Steve Tate lost control of the Big Canoe property when he ran afoul of the very same Internal Revenue Service that had busted up stills on the family property years before.

Charlene Terrell

"I have always identified with the mountain people and the old ways," says Big Canoeist Charlene Terrell. "I respect the hard life they endured years ago."

It was out of this respect that Charlene Terrell accepted an assignment to write a short pamphlet on the history of the peoples who lived in the area of Big Canoe before it became a gated community in 1973. As she plunged into her research, her respect deepened and grew. She worked patiently to trace living survivors of some of the early settlers, like the Disharoons.

Charlene Terrell with a copy of her book

Eight years later—six in research and two years of writing—she had finished. But *Wolfscratch Wilderness,* when completed, was no longer a small pamphlet. It had grown into a 700-page hardbound book.

The book is now in its third printing. It sells for $25 and is available at the General Store.

Through her thorough research, Charlene was able to recreate the life and times of a few key families that shaped the history and development of this area. She begins by recreating the life and family of a Cherokee Indian named Sconti, and follows her thread to the Potts, the Disharoons, and of course the Tates.

The story of Sconti is especially intriguing. He settled in Big Canoe at the beginning of the nineteenth century, and was one of the Cherokees removed to Oklahoma. But he made enough of an impact on the folklore and stories of the area that more than a century later, Sam Tate named his wooded retreat after him. The name remains associated with Big Canoe through Lake Sconti and Sconti clubhouse.

"I became friends with these people," Charlene explains, sitting in an easy chair at the Big Canoe Chapel, where she serves as administrative assistant. "I view them as part of my extended family. My goal was just to tell the story of the people who lived here before us, beginning with the Indians and working up to the present day.

"Some people look down on the mountain people as ignoramuses," she continues. "That is not the case at all. They are strong people, talented and determined. The heritage of this region is very rich."

Charlene's life in Big Canoe is centered on the chapel and its activities. When she and her husband Dave were thinking of moving up here, they visited the chapel for its Sunday service. Driving home, they were both quiet. Finally, Dave said, "there's something special there." At that time, the chapel was quite small—it has grown tremendously in the last 20 years, as the population of Big Canoe itself has grown. Nonetheless, they both felt a spiritual tie to the chapel—a tie that has only grown stronger for them since becoming residents.

Living in Big Canoe has not narrowed Charlene's focus in any way, however. Before retiring, she and Dave spent five months living in Malaga, Spain, learning to speak Spanish. Since moving to Big Canoe, they have taken trips to many of the countries in Central and South America. One of Charlene's dreams is to be able to visit a Castro-free Cuba.

Charlene has found the steady growth of Big Canoe to be exciting—and has been a part of it. The Terrell home on Grouse Gap is the third home they have owned and lived in since moving here.

"When we first moved here," she laughs, "the address list of the permanent residents barely filled a half a page. Now it takes seventeen."

Coming Together

As Big Canoe has grown, so has the opportunity to sponsor special events and activities as a community. Recognizing this, the Property Owners Association recently hired Sam Rothermel to develop and coordinate a year-long schedule of special events and organize a "Big Canoe Travel Club."

Sam had been a popular figure in the early years of Big Canoe, when he served as recreation director from 1973 to 1978.

As director of activities, Sam will oversee the annual events which have become a fixture at Big Canoe—Memorial Day, the 4th of July, Labor Day, and Oktoberfest—but also develop new activities in response to community requests.

Not all of the new activities will be limited to inside the gates at Big Canoe. On July 15 of this year, for example, Sam will lead a Big Canoe contingent to the Fox Theatre in downtown Atlanta. They will have dinner at Mary Mac's restaurant, take in the show, and then join a cast party to meet the star of the show, the son of Big Canoeists Ben and Rita Zoller.

Other activities will be held here at Big Canoe. The Georgia Ballet will visit on August 6th for a "camp performance." A series of nature presentations will be made in July and August. Over Labor Day weekend, there will be a dance billed as

Courtesy Debbie Pickett

Last year's symphony on the fairway was such a hit it led to an encore performance this summer

A skydiver drops to the ballpark during Labor Day festivities

"The Return of the Back-stabbers"—the Backstabbers being a local group that was popular at Big Canoe in the 1970's.

Atlanta radio personality Neil Boortz is scheduled to give a talk on September 23 at the Sconti.

Sam will also be leading groups of Big Canoeists on outings that take in games played by Atlanta's professional athletic teams.

The Travel Club is meant to provide Big Canoe property owners with "designer vacations" at discount prices. This fall, for example, Sam will lead a group on a hiking tour of the Swiss Alps. It will be a 9-day tour of alpine trails in central Switzerland, with a different hiking trail each day. The trails can be taken at a leisurely walk or as an exhilarating hike.

Other tours that may develop, if there is interest, include a trip to Biloxi, Mississippi; a cruise of the Caribbean; a walking tour in Vermont to catch the fall colors; a tour of Italy's Tuscany and Chianti regions; and visits to antique shows.

Special events are held in many venues around Big Canoe, from the Swim Club to Sconti to Broyles Center and the new ampitheater. Check the POA web site or *Smoke Signals* for more specific information about any program.

73

John's Mill

There are two fundamental differences between northern and southern cooking: wheat flour and corn meal. It simply isn't southern to try to make biscuits with flour that has not been ground in the South. The same is true for corn meal.

And if you are the kind of cook who insists on being as authentic as possible, it will not do to use either flour or corn meal you have purchased at the Piggly Wiggly. It needs to be stone ground the way it was 100 years ago.

Fortunately for Big Canoe enthusiasts, there is a mill about 30 minutes away that can supply all of the flour and corn meal anyone might need. It is called John's Mill after its owner, John Humphrey. John was the son and grandson of farmers, but the great-grandson of a miller. When he became an adult, he knew his true calling was to be a miller, too. He attributes this certainty to the beliefs in predestination of his Presbyte-

With the dam out back, John surveys his product line.
The wide strap on the right turns the mill.

rian background. So he bought an old mill on Scarecorn Creek just north of Hinton, restored the dam, and bought up all the equipment he needs to grind out all that we need for our daily bread: good flour and meal.

John works in a small log cabin, but he knows his craft—and he knows his cornbread.

Want the best cornbread possible? Follow the recipe that comes on his sack of corn meal. Then, after preheating the oven, turn it on broil. Place your cast iron skillet with the cornbread under the broiler and cook it a few minutes, until the top is brown. Then turn the oven down to 375° and cook the bread until done, about 25 minutes.

"The browned crust on top of the uncooked bread will keep the rising bubbles trapped in the bread," John explains, "instead of evaporating into the air. The result will be the fluffiest, airiest cornbread you ever ate."

When John decided to become a miller, he sought out a man who had worked as a miller all his life. He helped John buy his equipment and learn to use it. In this way, the old traditions of the business are still alive today in John.

John sells five products from his mill: wheat flour, yellow corn meal, white corn meal, honey, and dolls his wife makes out of cornhusks. He is open two days a week—Saturday from dawn until dusk, and Sunday from 1 p.m. until sunset. The mill is closed to the public the rest of the week.

If you want to buy any of John's products, you will be graciously welcomed. But John makes it very clear—he is in business. His mill is not a tourist spot nor a curiosity. It is a place of commerce. He has no patience for anyone who shows up during the week—or for gawkers out for a lark.

To get to John's Mill, drive westward on Highway 53 until you get to Hinton, about 10 miles beyond Jasper. Turn right on Carver Mill Road, then left on Dean Mill Road. Follow the dirt road until it dead ends at the mill.

John has no web site. He can't. The mill has no phone.

John's corn meal says it all. It's worth the trip.

The Bargain Trail

Is your blood type "O-shopping positive"? Do you need to go to a sale every now and then in order to feel alive? Don't worry—Big Canoe is right in the middle of the famed north Georgia Triangle.

Every weekend, thousands of pilgrims religously make their way to the North Georgia Premium Outlet Mall in Dawsonville, just south of the intersection of Highway 53 and Route 400. There they find a mecca of bargains—just about anything from designer clothing to Bose radio systems and Black and Decker tools.

At the other end of Highway 53, at the Calhoun exit of I-75, there is another collection of outlet stores. The triangle is completed by Warehouse Row in Chattanooga, just two hours to the north of Big Canoe—a short trip for true bargain lovers.

If you are looking for L.L. Bean type goods, try the Bargain Barn on Route 515 in Jasper. It is the best place in the region to buy thermal long underwear or camping equipment.

For more standard mall shopping, the two most convenient points are North Point Mall in Alpharetta (Georgia 400 and Haynes Bridge Road) and Riverstone Mall on I-575 in Canton.

An avenue of shops at the outlet mall

One developer is hard at work to bring shopping even closer. Land has been cleared for a shopping center at the corner of Route 53 and Steve Tate Highway. There is no word yet on what shops will be represented.

Local Hot Spots

Even in the middle of the north Georgia woods, it is possible to find good places to get a quick bite. It just takes a dash of the pioneer spirit to find some types of food. Here are some suggestions on sating various culinary appetites:

Lunch and dinner—the Crowe's Nest in Jasper can be loud, but otherwise serves good food. Their Mandarin orange salad is outstanding, with or without chicken. They also have good sandwiches and steaks—and marvelous ribs.

Further afield, but worth the trip, is Norman's Landing, just across Georgia 400 on Bethelview. Catering to the Lake Lanier crowd, Norman's also has great ribs, just 30 minutes from the Big Canoe gate. They also feature fresh fish and superb clam chowder—New England style.

Chinese—the Golden Palace at the intersection of Route 20 and Bethelview serves excellent Chinese food.

Breakfast and lunch—the Carriage House is a cute place to get a delicious bite in downtown Jasper. Try Jack's bread.

There are also Waffle Houses on both ends of 53—one in Jasper at Route 515, and the other in Dawsonville on Georgia 400 (just north of 53).

Barbeque—try Chad's, next to the Golden Palace at the intersection of Route 20 and Bethelview Road. Love those beans!

Pizza—the best pizza in Jasper is made at Olympia, at the corner of Route 53 and Burnt Mountain Road. If you are willing to travel any distance for great pizza, however, the place to go is Donatos on St. John's Parkway in Duluth. The rumor is that they may open a Donatos somewhere in north Alpharetta soon. If you are a thin crust lover, this is as good as it gets.

Mexican—El Azteca in Jasper is satisfying, but a great place for good Mexican food at inexpensive prices is the Fajita Grill on Route 9 in Alpharetta, just north of McFarland Road.

Fast food—Between Jasper (53 and 515) and Dawsonville (53 and 400) you can find almost everything imaginable.

Hidden Treasures

Got a lazy, rainy afternoon on your hands with nothing to do? Here are a few suggestions on how to shake the tedium out of your life. Each recommendation leads to a miniature treasure hidden here in Big Canoe.

• Visit the Robert H. Platt Botanical Museum on the second floor of the POA offices—the old Canoe Lodge. While a resident at Big Canoe, the late Robert Platt built a number of museum-quality exhibits portraying many of the natural inhabitants of Big Canoe—birds, wild turkeys, wild cats, and more. These superb exhibits are on display during the normal hours of operation of the POA.

The same area also has a small lending library of books.

• Check out the collection of gifts that have been presented to the Chapel in gratitude for the benevolent work it has done throughout the world. The display can be found on the lower level of the Broyles Center.

• While at the Broyles Center, pore through the library just down the hall. They have books and videos that have been donated by Big Canoeists over the year—so many that they had to move the library recently to a larger room. There are books on almost every subject.

• Visit the second floor of the General Store. Borrow a book—or rent a video you haven't seen before.

*A wild turkey
in a Robert Platt display*

E-Canoe

It is true that Big Canoe is a wilderness retreat sequestered in the mountains of north Georgia. But this in no way means that it is without the latest of modern technology.

Through cable TV's channel 12, Big Canoe keeps its residents up-to-date on what is happening—and where. The calendar of events is narrowcast 24 hours a day.

But Big Canoe is not just restricted to cablevision. At the same moment that residents are watching a troop of wild turkeys parade by their decks, they can be chatting with friends in Tulsa by e-mail, checking the stocks on Wall Street, or ordering books from Barnes and Noble—all through the computer internet.

In point of fact, Big Canoeists can even keep track of the latest news in Big Canoe by internet. The Big Canoe Company has its own web site, at www.bigcanoe.com. On it, you can tour homes that are currently on the market, preview lodging options, or check rates for holding a conference at the Chimneys.

The Property Owners Association also has a web site, at www. bigcanoepoa.org. Check it out for the menu of this week's Wednesday night dinner at the Sconti—or to download the latest regulations from the Architectural Control Committee.

To see the dogs or cats being placed by Animal Rescue, check the web as well—at www.bcdogs.mindspring.com.

In addition, DSL lines will be available in Big Canoe for faster service by mid-fall.

Many Big Canoeists have found the web allows them to work at home, with the wild turkeys and deer, instead of downtown—with the sharks.

The Ball Park

One of the most popular amenities at Big Canoe is the ballpark at the base of the Lake Petit dam.

Tucked in a flat piece of land between the dam, the water plant, and Buckskull Hollow, the ballpark offers many recreational possibilities. One is a walking/jogging path that inscribes the circumference of the field. The path is one-quarter of a mile long and flat, enabling joggers to run their daily mile.

Several picnic tables near the parking lot make it possible for spouses to relax and enjoy a snack or cup of coffee while their mates build up a sweat working out. They also make a good place for mothers to chat while their children romp on the outdoor play equipment.

An outdoor basketball court can be used for a full fledged game—or just to shoot hoops. One resident of the East Lake neighborhood walks daily to the post office to collect his mail, then stops at the ball park to shoot hoops on his way back—a

round trip of four miles!

A ball diamond and a volley ball court complete the attractions. The facilities are open to all Big Canoeists. Bring your own balls.

Gene Risoldi shoots hoops; a game of volleyball heats up

Preserving Nature

"The number one consideration in all management planning in Big Canoe is the preservation of our natural resources," says Nancy Zak, executive vice president of the Big Canoe Company. "We work hard to be stewards of this land, and to offer so many people the chance to call this wonderful spot in nature their home."

Preserving the natural enchantment of Big Canoe is a task that requires much vigilance. But it is not something that the Big Canoe Company wants to leave to chance. It is built into the way they approach development—and into the covenants which govern land usage.

Before the first home was ever built in Big Canoe, a large portion of the 7,600 acres comprising the planned community were protected from development by being allocated as "green space." No homes or buildings can ever be built in these sections. They have been set aside to preserve the natural beauty that graces so much of Big Canoe. Some green spaces are quite large, such as Nature Valley. Others are quite small. But all of them contribute to the magic of the land, and to the natural habitats of the animals living here.

It is not just

A cinnamon fern

Bryant McDaniel

green space that protects nature in Big Canoe, however. The same care guides Big Canoe Company as it lays out roads and new home-sites.

"We believe in keeping tree cutting and earth moving to a minimum," Nancy continues. "We walk potential homesites before they are platted, making sure that roads do not interfere with any special features, and that homes will blend in with the terrain, not disrupt it. Our goal is to preserve the essence of what we have."

In order to keep the natural drainage of the many creeks and draws in the woods unchanged, the roads in Big Canoe have been built without curbs or gutters. Road widths are also kept at a minimum, to prevent having to cut down any more trees than necessary and to reduce disturbing hillsides with excessive grading.

An important aspect of keeping Big Canoe natural is controlling the impact of buildings, roads, and other improvements on our visual environment. This philosophy led to the adoption of extensive architectural guidelines. "The guidelines are designed to help all man-made structures blend in with their natural surroundings," observes Bryant McDaniel, an early general manager of Big Canoe who now serves as vice-president of development. Toward this end, most of the paint and stain colors permitted for the outside of buildings are natural shades.

This approach has proven to be a major key to the success of Big Canoe: emphasize our natural surroundings, not the homes and other structures. The decision to preserve the trout streams of the Wildcat neighborhood as a series of interlocking parks, instead of building the planned golf course, is an excellent example of The Big Canoe Company's commitment to preserving the environment for everyone's enjoyment.

It is for this reason that the covenants also restrict tree cutting on private property. No flowering trees or shrubs, and no trees under six inches in trunk diameter, may be cut or trimmed unless they are within 10 feet of a home. No lawns (and no lawn mowers) are permitted in Big Canoe, for the same reason. People move to Big Canoe to enjoy the woods.

Bryant explains that it has often been a fight to keep Big Canoe the way it is. "Over the years, we have worked closely with a number of government agencies to promote an understanding of low-impact development in mountainous terrain. Fortunately, we have had excellent cooperation from the officials in both Dawson and Pickens counties."

Water drainage is a good example. "County rules are set up to direct storm water away from property. We want storm water to seep in evenly throughout the forest, so it feeds the woods and springs and creeks."

Nancy adds that the Big Canoe Compnay seeks to work with the natural topography of the land, and—in some cases, tries to restore prior conditions. In developing McDaniel Meadows, for example, they cut out some first-generation trees to replicate the fields and pastures that had been cultivated for more than a century by the McElroys and the Cochrans.

Nancy Zak

"These woods are our most precious asset," Nancy concludes. "It is our mission to preserve and protect them, even while providing facilities for people to live here and enjoy them."

83

Smokey Says

The biggest asset of Big Canoe is its trees. It is also its greatest potential source for danger; if a forest fire were to ignite and spread, the enchantment of Big Canoe might be gone for a long time.

For this reason, a big sign of Smokey the Bear stands just inside each gate, reminding residents and visitors to Big Canoe that there is no room for carelessness with fire of any kind.

Usually, the danger of fire is low, due to the high quantity—and frequency of rain—that we receive in north Georgia. But there can be dry spells, and then the danger can grow.

According to Dean Cantrell, head of Big Canoe security, fire, and rescue, Big Canoe's fire protection has been the best in the area for years—and is constantly getting better.

Last year, for example, the Propety Owners Association built a fire station on POA property across the road from the north gate. It leases it—along with ambulances and fire trucks—to Dawson County. In return, the county staffs and maintains the station—Station Six—of which Cantrell is the captain.

By joining with the county in this way, the POA not only saves operating money, but also improves the quality of its fire service and rescue operations. "Dawson County rotates its personnel every three months," Dean explains. "We have very few incidents here, so our people do not get much practical experience, compared to those working in Dawsonville. When people who have been working in town are assigned out here, we benefit from their experience."

Dean also explains that Dawson County provides 120 hours of training each year for every member of the Big Canoe security staff that patrols the community—free. Fourteen members of his staff receive this education.

At least two security vehicles patrol Big Canoe at all times. If there is an emergency, the closest vehicle responds to the call, while the other goes to the north gate to lead the fire department vehicles to the scene.

Big Canoe still maintains fire engines in stations throughout the community, and is able to use them for first response to any fire, and to support the Dawson firefighters. Security team members are all volunteer members of the fire department.

Cantrell says that one of the strengths of Big Canoe's fire protection is its water supply and distribution system. "If one storage tank is drained, we can switch to another in a matter of seconds and keep pumping."

Fire safety is actually built in from the beginning. "Big Canoe has 300 to 400 fire hydrants," Dean says. "As a new neighborhood is opened, the fire hydrants are one of the first things the developer installs. I know a lot of people take fire hydrants for granted, but we don't. Those hydrants give us the water to save homes—and lives."

Dean Cantrell
Briefs Robin Henderson

Inside the Gates

The natural setting of the mountains and lakes create the serenity of life inside Big Canoe.   But there is another factor that is quite important in maintaining the retreat-like quality of Big Canoe: the efforts of the POA's security team.

The work of security is twofold: to make sure that only people invited to Big Canoe are able to enter, and to help residents and guests encountering emergencies and distress.

The first challenge is addressed at the two entrance gates, where one-third of Dean Cantrell's security, fire, and rescue staff is assigned. Security personnel check credentials on everyone entering the community. Big Canoe residents are waved through if driving a car with a proper sticker; everyone else must stop and register. Guests are cleared rapidly if the residents they are visiting have called the appropriate gate in advance. Otherwise, they must wait until the guard calls and verifies the visit.

The second challenge is addressed by the rest of the security staff, as calls come in. "Let's say a resident has a flat tire along Wilderness Parkway, and they call the gate on their cell phone for help," Dean says. "We'll dispatch one of the guards patrol-

The North Gate

ing the neighborhood to go help that person."

Other calls commonly received from residents include reports of trash on the roads, loud music being played in a neighborhood, other distracting noises, and reports of deer or bears trying to get into houses. The security patrols are equipped and trained to handle them all.

10-year veteran Betty Griffith checks in a visitor

They are also ready to handle more serious problems, such as medical emergencies. As a result of cooperation with Dawson County, an emergency 911 call from anywhere in Big Canoe—either county—will give the security team the address where the problem is occurring. "Even if a resident is able only to pick up the phone, dial 911, and then hang up, we will know instantly their address—and we will respond immediately." Dean says.

The security patrols are well trained and well equipped. Each truck carries oxygen and a portable defibrolator, as well as other medical supplies.

One other important function of the security patrols is to help everyone driving in Big Canoe—construction workers, repair trucks, and guests, as well as residents—maintain the speed limit of 25 miles per hour. "We are not trying to create a police state," Dean insists. "We just want Big Canoe to be a safe environment for everyone."

First tickets are written warnings. Repeat offenses result in fines. "We're just trying to slow folks down," Dean adds, "not trying to see how many tickets we can write."

Clearing the Way

It's no simple task to keep all the vital "arteries" of Big Canoe clear and unclogged, particularly after a heavy storm. It is an ongoing chore, the work of the roads, paths, and grounds maintenance crew headed by Toby Jones.

Toby's staff handles every odd task that comes along with professionalism and equanamity—from uprighting pontoon boats that have been flipped by winds to picking up litter along the roadways left by careless people. They are also responsible for removing the bodies of suicidal squirrels who leap in front of moving vehicles.

Toby's biggest challenge is maintaing the 80+ miles of roads within Big Canoe. "We try to repave 10 miles a year," he says, adding that his crew is also busy patching potholes as they appear. But the work on the roadways does not stop there. His troops mow the shoulders along the roads and clean out drainage ditches.

"The biggest challenge to me is scheduling," Toby, a longtime veteran of the POA support staff, observes. "We do not know from day to day what might come up—or whether the weather will let us work on it."

Take the ice storm that hit Big Canoe this winter, toppling trees throughout the forest. Toby's crew sprung into

A road crew cleans drainage ditches

action immediately. "In a situation like that, we always start by clearing a path so that the rescue vehicles can get through, should there be an emergency. Then we clear the rest of the roadways. It takes weeks to clean up all the debris after some storms."

Another important job Toby's staff is responsible for is keeping the hiking trails in top shape. "We walk all the trails in Big Canoe at least once a month, to make sure they are in good condition," Toby says. If trees have fallen over the path, they will be cleared. If bridges need repair, a crew will be dispatched to fix them. Trash will be picked up and disposed.

During the summer, Toby's crew is also responsible for maintaining the landscaping around the gates and the various community buildings. In all, he has a staff of 10 full-time and two part-time people to keep the roads and grounds in good shape.

10-year veteran Jewell Lingerfelt trolls for litter

Building bridges is part of the work of Toby's crews. Right, Toby shows that Big Canoe is "carved in stone"

Buying In

The fateful moment arrives. A couple decides to buy a home-site or a home in Big Canoe. This brings up a whole new question: what is the best way to proceed?

For most people, the answer is Big Canoe Realty. Located in the heart of Wolfscratch Village, Big Canoe Realty has been a part of the community since it opened in 1972, and is a driving force behind the growth of Big Canoe.

"We aren't just selling homes to people," says Paul Hanks, vice-president of sales and marketing for Big Canoe Company. "We are helping people become our neighbors, a part of our community. We are sales professionals in every sense of the word who treat every one who wants us to show them a house or a homesite as a friend."

As new neighborhoods are developed, the homesites are put up for sale through Big Canoe Realty. They are purchased either by builders, who build a "spec" home on them, or by future residents of Big Canoe.

In buying a homesite, it is important to consider a lot of factors: view, neighborhood, cost, and the challenge of building the kind of home

Jim Francis and Adaline Cullen show a Chestnut Knoll home to buyers Joanne and Paul Pattek

you want on the lot you have picked.

All of the Big Canoe sales professionals are trained to give you the answers and guidance you need. There is no "hard sell" in Big Canoe. The sales approach is as relaxed as the community itself.

Once you buy a homesite, the staff will be more than willing to put you in touch with a top notch builder—if your plans call for building immediately. There are currently seven builders who participate in the Big Canoe building program.

Paul Hanks

Even if you wait for several years before deciding to build, the Big Canoe sales professionals will be more than willing to guide you correctly at that time.

In addition to homesites, however, the Big Canoe real estate team sells homes—either "spec" homes just constructed by a builder or an "older" home now being resold. In Big Canoe, "older" homes range in age from one to 27 years.

Actually, even though Big Canoe has spawned an entire industry of real estate companies in the area, Big Canoe Realty sells more homes each year than all the rest of the agencies combined. It only makes sense: the members of the Big Canoe team are the ones who know the residents of the community best.

"We are service oriented," says Paul Hanks. "A realtor down the street just wants to sell you a home. It doesn't matter to him if it is inside or outside the gates. We sell Big Canoe—the whole experience. So our efforts never stop."

Being a part of the development company, Big Canoe Realty has its pulse on current and future plans. The Big Canoe Company has recently inaugurated a new concept—carefree family homes on condominium homesites. The first grouping is under construction at Chestnut Knoll, with spectacular views of Creek golf course, Lake Disharoon, and the mountains. The homes, selling in the $220,000 to $280,000 range, have touched a very responsive chord among buyers.

"Our close connection with the development team is also a good reason why current home owners should list with us when it comes time to build another home in Big Canoe," Paul says. "New offerings such as Chestnut Knoll, along with all that we do to promote the community, draw many people to Big Canoe—but not all of the buyers will necessarily purchase a new product. They may well buy your house instead."

Another such connection that pays off in homes sold is the link Big Canoe enjoys with *Southern Living* magazine. Three years ago, *Southern Living* sponsored an "Idea House" in the Wedgewood neighborhood, overlooking Cherokee #7. Last year, "Holly Springs" in the Audubon at Sconti neighborhood was featured. These homes brought thousands of people to Big Canoe, plus made readers throughout the South aware of Big Canoe as "a premier mountain community."

In addition, the realty team has recently begun presenting "virtual tours" of selected homes for sale on its web site, www.bigcanoe.com.

Paul heads "a great team" of 17 sales professionals, each one thoroughly dedicated to selling the Big Canoe experience.

Paul Hanks (left front) leads a meeting of his sales staff

Building a Home

As new settlers bought property in the Wolfscratch region, they had to build themselves a home—anywhere from a rough one-room log cabin to a clapboard house. Perhaps their need to build has hung in the aura of Big Canoe for all these years, but one thing is certain—part of the enchantment of the place is the almost mystical compulsion to build a home. Some long-time residents have actually built three or four homes since first coming to Big Canoe.

Let's face it—building a new home can either be a frustrating or an exhilarating process. To make the process easier, the Big Canoe Company has established a "builders program," to guarantee new residents a wide selection of builders, all of them dedicated to quality and economy, to choose among. All of them are well acquainted with the covenants governing building in Big Canoe, and have mastered the intricacies of building new homes in mountainous terrain.

The stories of each of these builders follow.

A tradesman works on a new Timberstone home

Randy and Nick Schiltz (top) check out the stone work of James Ray, right, and his helper Henry Bridges

Nick C. Schiltz, Inc.

"The key to building a great home is communication," says Nick Schiltz who, with his son Randy, has been building homes in Big Canoe for six years—including the 1997 *Southern Living* "Idea House" in the Wedgewood neighborhood. In fact, the team of Nick and Randy have been named by the magazine as one of the top 100 builders in the South.

"We are small and hands on," Nick adds. "We do not bite off more than we can chew." For this reason, the Schiltzes only have four to five homes under construction at the same time.

"We are on our job sites every day, which let's us be present whenever decisions need to be made," Randy says. He adds that they make sure to keep their customers up to date on the progress of their new homes.

Nick insists on building to codes tougher than he encountered in Fulton County, where he built homes before moving his focus to Big Canoe. "I live here in Big Canoe," he says with a laugh. "That is part of our guarantee on all of our homes—our customers know exactly where to find me."

Castell Home Construction

"Quality comes first," says Claude Castell, a native of France who now builds exclusively in Big Canoe.

To make sure it does, Claude and his partner George Kudrick supervise every step of the building process personally, from pouring the foundation to setting the windows to installing the finishes touches.

"If a window isn't set right," George explains, "it may never work right."

Claude, who studied architecture in France, has been building homes in Big Canoe since 1989—some of them his own designs.

Claude and George

George joined him earlier this year. He had been vice-president of the Bank of North Georgia in Jasper; as such, he had been directly involved in building in Big Canoe for eight years.

By working together, Claude and George are a team that can solve any problem in building and financing a home.

"Our goal is to build a new home in no more than 8 months," says George, "and to build 8 to 10 new homes a year. That's the maximum we can build and still be sure that every home is being built right."

Claude, who has lived in Big Canoe since 1992—refers to himself as an "interpreter" who takes the dreams of his customers and translates them into wood and stacked stone. "My goal," he says, "is to make sure that each step in building a house is done right, so there will be no problems later on."

Crown Construction

"Our goal is to offer our customers the best values and most efficient service in Big Canoe," declares Paul Castell, president of Crown Construction. "We are a full service construction company," he adds. "We build new homes—not just conventional homes, but also timber homes and log homes—and we also do remodeling through Summit Remodeling."

In fact, Paul describes his company as "a building system." He has put together a construction team that can handle every phase of the building process, from architectural design to landscaping. In this way, he can maintain continuity in any building project he undertakes.

"It can take longer to erect a new home in Big Canoe than in Atlanta," Paul states. "With our experience and efficiencies, we try to keep our building time to a minimum."

Paul has been building in Big Canoe for six years—and now builds only in Big Canoe. Like many of the builders, he likes Big Canoe so much that he lives here himself. In fact, he is building himself a new home—with office attached.

Paul Castell checks specs on a home in progress

Crown Construction builds five to ten homes a year. Two are built on speculation; the rest are custom built for the site owner. Paul's price range is from $300,000 to $1 million plus.

"Most of our business comes from referrals from well-satisfied customers," Paul adds. "That is our main goal as we start each new home: to end up with a satisfied homeowner."

Fireside Properties, Inc.

"Every home should have a woman's input," says Brenda Young of Fireside Properties. In her case, she brings an artistic flair to the design side of homebuilding; she has degrees in art and design.

Husband Bart worked 28 years with IBM and took advantage of "the last of the great buyouts" to exchange his suit for work clothes.

Together, they aim to build "elegant homes with a country feel."

That means incorporating a lot of stonework on the interior of the home—not just in fireplaces but also in entire walls. They put marble inlays in the heart of their hardwood flooring and add extra trim throughout the house to accentuate the elegance.

"We believe in making our homes liveable," Brenda emphasizes. Toward this end, they build oversized master bedrooms.

"We are on-the-job builders," adds Bart. "We check out each job site every day, to keep tabs on the quality of workmanship. We settle for nothing but the best."

Bart and Brenda have been building in Big Canoe for two years, ever since they first visited and fell in love with it.

"We were extremely impressed by the people at Big Canoe Realty," Brenda adds. "There is such a warm and cozy atmosphere up here. We are planning to build a home for ourselves and move up here as soon as we can."

Jim LaBonte Builders, Inc.

"I'm a happy builder. I love building here in Big Canoe."
Why is Jim LaBonte so happy?

In part, it might be because he lives in Big Canoe, and he can find a Jim LaBonte home just about everywhere he turns. "I build about 25 new homes in Big Canoe each year," he states, adding that he also builds the same number of new homes in other nearby communities.

It might be that he built Holly Springs, the 1999 *Southern Living* "plan of the month" home in the Audubon at Sconti neighborhood. More than 15,000 people toured the home while it was being shown last fall.

It might also be the realization that Jim has traveled a long way from the time he first arrived in Atlanta as a salesman for a large national home builder. He worked his way up through the ranks to become a top executive.

When the company decided to pull out of Atlanta, Jim went into business for himself. He has been building custom homes ever since.

His secret? "I communicate with every customer. I have to satisfy each one—my future livelihood depends on their referrals."

Jim LaBonte inspecting Holly Springs

Timberstone Properties, Inc.

"We are design-conscious," says Mike Spangler, head of Timberstone Properties and a trained architect himself. "By the time we start pouring a foundation, we know the real priorities of the customer, and have designed a home to fit their needs perfectly."

For a current project, for example, Mike designed the home around an art collection, building lighted recesses and alcoves throughout the house. In another case, he built the home to take maximum advantage of its location along Cherokee #2.

"We take the idea of 'custom building' as far as we can. No two of our homes ever turn out alike, either inside or out."

Mike likes the challenge of building in Big Canoe, and builds nowhere else. For one home, he had his crew move three dozen

mountain laurel and six wild azalea trees, healing them in what will be the front yard. All but one of the trees survived the transplanting, and the front walk now wends its way through a delightful bosque—the perfect entrance to a lakefront home.

"We make sure that every square foot of the home is usable," Mike adds. The price range of a Timberstone home is from $450,000 to $650,000.

In the four years since starting in Big Canoe, Mike has built 11 to 12 homes. "We are carefully expanding," he says, "but have no intention of biting off more than we can chew."

Design Control

In building in Big Canoe, all builders must be approved by the Architectural Control Department of the Property Owners Association, and must obey all of its guidelines and restrictions. In this way, the architectural continuity of Big Canoe is guaranteed and preserved.

To install propane for heating and cooking, for instance, a builder is required to either bury the tank or screen it from view. No exposed concrete driveways or sidewalks are permitted; only black top may be used. Only the fewest number of trees may be removed to build a house; whenever possible, trees should be transplanted elsewhere on the property instead of being cut down.

No brick or vinyl siding may be used on exterior facings; stone and wood siding are the preferred choices. Only paint colors that help homes blend into the natural environment are permitted; authorized colors are listed by brand and shade.

Landscaping plans as well as all blueprints must be submitted for approval before a contractor can first break ground. The same procedures must be followed for remodeling.

What a Great Idea

Between the demands of the terrain and the desires of the homeowners, every home built in Big Canoe is something of an innovation. Here are some of the great ideas the Big Canoe builders have come up with in trying to satisfy these needs creatively, economically, and stylishly.

A tradesman assembles a custom built bannister, left; a walk through pantry is tucked behind the kitchen

Instead of ties, this retaining wall is made of giant stones

Kudzu Wars

Many people think the only wars fought on Southern soil were the War of Independence, the War of 1812, the Indian Wars, and the Civil War. These people have never heard of kudzu.

Kudzu is a creeping vine that is found throughout the South, most commonly along roadways—such as Steve Tate Highway. It drapes like crepe paper over pine trees, eventually killing them. It climbs over stop signs, fences, and old sheds; it invades gardens, abandoned cars, and anything else left untended during the summer. If you have ever lived near it, you are at war with it—and you are losing.

Kudzu is not native to the South. It comes from Japan, where it grows in the mountains and is known as *kuzu.* It was brought to the South during the Depression to held stop erosion. At that time, it was hailed as the plant that would save the South. Ten years later, it had become known as "the plant that ate the South."

Since there are no natural enemies of kudzu in America, there is nothing to check its growth. And its growth is speedy, to say the least. Some folks claim kudzu can grow a foot a day. As a result, it devours Dixie faster than Godzilla can swallow Tokyo.

The thing about kudzu is its roots, which are remarkably deep. In Japan, they are treasured as a source of aphrodisia. In Georgia, they are cursed, because the only way to kill kudzu is to dig out every bit of root and destroy it. Otherwise, it will repropagate itself.

It is difficult to find kudzu within Big Canoe, thanks to a concerted effort is keep the menace outside the gates. But it is hard to drive very far from Big Canoe without encountering it.

Just remember: if life gives you nothing but kudzu, pick the blossoms and make kudzu jelly from them. It's go-o-o-od.

The Chimneys

Ann Young

It is the perfect setting for a corporate retreat—or a memorable wedding. The Chimneys Conference Center is right in the heart of Wolfscratch Village, yet looks serenely out over the majestic Lake Sconti.

Inside, there are three rooms that can be rented for any kind of activity—the Ivy, large enough to hold a dance contest; the Laurel, cozy and intimate, perfect for a board meeting; and the Tavern, ideal for a reunion. Or put them all together for a large gathering, such as a wedding.

Each room has been professionally decorated by Big Canoe-ist Melissa Ward. The Chimneys, with a cozy fireplace in each room, is a conference center with personality and warmth.

If the weather cooperates, you can spill out onto the massive porches and patio overlooking Lake Sconti.

Whatever your function, you can count on expert planning and coordination from Ann Young and her capable staff. Need catering? The Chimneys has professional facilities and can recommend several area caterers. Want to book five rental cottages to house your guests? No problem—Ann's staff also handles booking house rentals. Want tee times for everyone in your party? It can be arranged.

"Our goal is to make sure our guests enjoy every moment inside Big Canoe," says Ann. "We are focused on their total stay, not just the time they spend inside our building."

Ann is also Big Canoe's roving ambassador. "I spend a lot of my time in Atlanta," she says, selling companies on the advantages of having their next conference at Big Canoe. In fact, she is constantly looking for ways to bring new people into Big Canoe. "I'm not just trying to book conventions," she says. "I'm trying to introduce people to Big Canoe. I figure that once they come here for a convention or a function, they will want to come back—most people do."

Toward this end, Ann is always on the lookout for programs or activities that can be scheduled into the Chimneys—classes, retreats, or symposia—and expose a new set of people to the charms of Big Canoe.

The conference center has gone through numerous transformations since the beginning of Big Canoe. It is named for the two chimneys which are still standing in the patio between the conference center and the sales office. Those two chimneys are all that is left of the home that Steve and Lucille Tate lived in. It burned down in 1959, shortly after Steve died. Lucille then renovated an old barn, renamed it Barndwell, and moved into it, until she sold the property. That structure became the offices of the Property Owners Association, sometimes called the Canoe Lodge.

The Chimneys was one of the first new buildings built after the opening of Big Canoe. It acted as headquarters for the real estate team. Later on, it became a restaurant and gathering place for the residents. A few years ago, it was refurbished as a conference center.

A Tale of 2 Counties

One of the more interesting oddities about Big Canoe is that it is split in two between Pickens and Dawson counties. The line bisects Lake Petit from east to west, a little north of the dam. Except for a finger of land west of the Nature Valley, everything north of the line lies in Dawson County; everything else lies in Pickens County.

One of the first steps all new property owners should take is to ascertain whether they are residents of Dawson or Pickens county. The county of your residence will not affect your life inside Big Canoe, but it will make a difference outside.

If you have children in the public school system, they will attend classes in Jasper if you live in Pickens County—and in Dawsonville if you live in Dawson County, although Dawson parents have the option of sending their kids to Pickens schools.

In Pickens County, you can get auto tags at the court house on Main Street in Jasper. You can also register to vote there— or at the library, just south of Cove Road on Burnt Mountain.

In Dawson County, tags can be purchased at the new courthouse just north of Dawsonville's main square. To register to vote, you must go back to the original courthouse, right in the center of the square. In either county, they will tell you where to vote when you register.

Driver's licenses can be obtained by residents of either county at a facility run by the state troopers on Georgia 400 just north of Route 369.

The marble courthouse in Jasper

The P.O.A.

It is not just enough to conceive a vision, build swimming pools and golf courses, and then sell lots to eager homeowners. A community like Big Canoe can only thrive if the amenities are maintained, the programs are well-implemented, and the homeowners actually enjoy living here.

Keeping the enchantment a living presence in Big Canoe is the work of the Property Owners Association, a group composed of all Big Canoe property owners, including the developer, the Big Canoe Company. The POA owns and maintains all of the community amenities and common areas.

Big Canoe is unique among developed communities in that the developer does not control the POA. Home and lot owners have as strong a voice as Big Canoe Company in issues that come before the POA. Maintaining the vision of Big Canoe is a shared responsibility.

The day-to-day fulfillment of this responsibility is the task of Troy Ledbetter, who has been general manager of the POA for three years.

Troy, who has been part of the Big Canoe experiment as long as anyone—he started as a security guard in 1971—says the vision is being well maintained and implemented.

"What is happening in Big Canoe today, after 30 years of

Troy Ledbetter

development, is extremely close to what Tom Cousins envisioned 30 years ago. Everyone who has played a part in shaping the community ought to be proud of what it has become."

Ledbetter gives credit to every segment of the community—the Developer, the POA staff, and the property owners—to making Big Canoe the success it is.

"The POA board consists of six members. Three serve at the request of the Developer, and three are elected by the property owners. As a result, no section of the community can dictate what will happen to another section. We have to work in cooperation and agreement."

The work of the POA is heavily supported by a collection of committees, advising the general manager on issues ranging from the lakes and fishing to the roads and trails. "We aren't run by the committees, but we listen closely to what they say, and depend greatly on their advice and guidance. We would love to see everyone in the community get involved through one committee or another. The committees are the strength of the community," Troy adds.

In addition to running all of the amenities in Big Canoe—a challenge which is examined in detail in articles throughout this book—the POA has the task of interacting with the governments of both Dawson and Pickens counties.

"We have an excellent relationship with both counties," Troy comments, "and I expect that to continue." He cites the arrangement he struck with Dawson County to provide fire and rescue services to Big Canoe in exchange for a fire station and equipment on POA property as an example of this cooperation. "It saves us a lot of money each year—and improves both our fire and rescue service—and Dawson County's."

The POA spends $2.5 million a year on a payroll of 80 full-time employees and 40 part-time employess in the summer.

Troy says that his goal is to make the amenities the best they possibly can be, "and to make sure that the POA is serving the community in the best way it can in everything we do.

"I try to make a difference."

Settling In

Whether you buy a home or build one, the rites of passage into Big Canoe involve one experience every homeowner shares: moving.

No matter how many times you have moved before, moving to Big Canoe is apt to be different. The major difference is that the roads in Big Canoe are hilly, narrow, and winding. So are the driveways. So, even though a 48-foot tractor-trailer moving van may be able to turn into the north gate, it is dubious that it can make it all the way to your front door. Even if it can make it to the foot of your driveway, the entire load may have to be offloaded into a smaller truck in order to deliver it the last 100 feet.

If a moving company has to send out extra crew members and a truck at the last moment, you are going to pay a lot of extra expenses—and be delayed in settling in. So be sure your moving company understands the specific requirements of moving into your new Big Canoe home, ahead of time.

Another factor you ought to consider when first moving in is to familiarize yourself with the lay of the land on your lot. Lots in Big Canoe are not squares or rectangles bordered by sidewalks and alleys. They are trapezoidal at best. Ask for a copy of the plat and walk the boundaries of your lot, so you know where they are. Figure out where the septic system is—and where the propane tank is, if there is one. If the previous owner or builder cannot supply this information, the Architectural Control Office probably can. Call them at 268-3394.

Once you are settled in, you will probably want to invite relatives and friends to come visit your new home. If you do, be sure to give them clear directions so that they can find their way from the front gate to your residence. And don't forget to call the appropriate gate to let them know you are going to have visitors. Otherwise, your guests will have to cool their heels while the gate calls to confirm that your guests are welcomed.

Bullet Bob Turley

Bob Turley was standing on the deck of his home on Tanager Way, looking out toward Lake Petit and Wet Mountain beyond. He turned and said, "We love it here. Every night the deer come down to the lake to get a drink."

In a cryptic sense, that comment sums up Bob Turley. He is a legend among baseball legends, as well as a highly successful business executive. Yet what draws him and his wife Carolyn to Big Canoe is its quiet simplicity—the opportunity to commune with the deer every night at dusk.

Turley was a star pitcher for the New York Yankees during the Casey Stengel years. He played with Mickey Mantle and Roger Maris. But he starred in his own right. In 1958, he won 21 games for the Yankees, won the Cy Young award, was named Most Valuable Player in the World Series, and won the Hitchcock Belt as the Professional Athlete of the year. But when asked to name the greatest thrills from his baseball days, Bob

Bullet Bob with Cy Young

replies: "The awards and trophies were all wonderful, but there was never a thrill that could beat the day when I was 18 years old, a kid from East St. Louis, standing on the diamond of the old ballpark of the St. Louis Browns, having just made the team."

Turley got the nickname "Bullet Bob" from an article in *Look* magazine that used a device invented to measure the speed of bullets to rate the speed of his blazing fastball. "It was clocked at 98 mph, but that was as the ball crossed the plate. Today's radar guns measure the speed as the pitcher releases the ball."

Turley went with the Browns to Baltimore, when they became the Orioles, and then was traded to the Yankees in 1954. He spent eight years pitching for what he calls "the greatest baseball organization of all time," and then served as a pitching coach for a year with Boston. He was asked to coach for Houston in 1965, but decided after spring training to head to California, where he had an executive sales position awaiting him with the Wonder Bread bakery group. En route, he stopped to see a friend in Atlanta. "My friend was in the securities business and suggested that I stay with him a while and try my hand selling stocks. So I did. The first week I made $1,000. By the second week, I was up to $5,000. So I stayed."

Bob, Carolyn, and Black Bart

He calls his success in business a "fairy tale story." In 1977, he was part of a group that formed a company that eventually became Primerica Financial, buying out numerous financial companies. It is now known as Citigroup.

In 1973, his friend Tom Cousins told him about a tract of land he was developing in North Georgia, so Bob came up to inspect Big Canoe on its opening day. He used the facilities regularly for business conferences and getaways over the years, then spent a summer. He and Carolyn now spend every summer watching the deer come down to the lake to drink.

Clean Mountain Water

A dependable source of water is a key element in supporting a community the size of Big Canoe. In the early years, a system of wells provided the water we drank. By 1996, however, Big Canoe Utilities, Inc. had completed construction of a surface water treatment plan and had brought in United Water Services, under contract, to operate the water and waste systems.

All of the community's water now comes from Lake Petit, which contains about two billion gallons of water. "We currently pump between 250,000 and 500,000 gallons a day to meet the drinking water needs of Big Canoe," says Bobby Smallwood, head of United Water's operation. The water treatment plant is capable of processing 1 million gallons a day.

The biggest water treatment problem today? In the last few years, it has been the need to remove the unusually large algae bloom from Lake Petit's water so that it does not slow down filtration. In most years, the cold winter weather kills the algae.

Waste water collected from properties in the core area of the community is treated at a secondary treatment facility, then pumped to a final filtering plant before the purified water is returned to nature. Most homes in Big Canoe have private septic systems.

Bobby Smallwood checks out a water filtration unit to ensures that Big Canoe's drinking water meets state requirements

Big Canoe Trivia Test

How much do you know about Big Canoe? Here are a few questions that might stump you, even if you have lived here 27 years. The answers can be found on page 114.

1. What is the name of the island in Lake Petit?

2. Who holds the record for the lowest 18-hole round on the Big Canoe golf courses?

3. Why did the Big Canoe Chapel build a separate belltower for its bell?

4. What is the significance of the name John Warren Ockhamto?

5. When Big Canoe was named, what name for the property, suggested by a consulting firm, was outright rejected by Tom Cousins?

6. The average annual rainfall in the city of Atlanta is 50 inches. How many inches of precipitation does Big Canoe receive in an average year?

7. Where is the town of Holcomb, Georgia—and how is it important to Big Canoe?

8. What type of motor vehicles are not allowed anywhere in Big Canoe?

9. How many residences have now been built in Big Canoe?

10. Why is the north gate called "Gate #3?"

11. What grows even faster than kudzu?

12. (See picture at right.) You know *what* it is, but just *where* is it?

113

The Envelope, Please

The answers to the Big Canoe Trivia Test are:

1. Eagle Island.

2. Troy Ledbetter holds the record of 65.

3. The bell was too heavy for the original belltower, built in the steeple of the chapel. Whenever it rang, its support beams would creak. So a new belltower was built to solve the problem.

4. It is the name inscribed on the face of the grandfather clock in the Ivy Room of the Chimneys Conference Center. Presumably, the clock was presented to Mr. Ockhamto as a gift many years ago.

5. Valkadia, a neologoistic collision between the Norse word Valhalla, meaning "the hall of slain heroes," and Arcadia, a rustic, isolated region in the Peloponnesian mountains of ancient Greece.

6. Believe it or not, 72 to 75 inches of rain fall in the Enchanted Land every year.

7. Holcomb, Georgia is the intersection of Steve Tate Highway and Route 53. It is the nearest town to Big Canoe. The Holcomb Corner Store on the right side of 53 as you turn west from Steve Tate—now the Foothills construction headquarters—was the primary clue to the identity of the community.

8. Under the rules and regulations of the POA, motorcycles, motor bikes, and motor scooters are not permitted to be driven anywhere inside Big Canoe.

9. Including multi-residential units as well as single-family homes, the total was 1430 homes at the start of 2000.

10. There once was a "Gate #2," just south of the golf maintenance entrance. It has been permanently closed.

11. The only thing that grows faster than kudzu is the latest rumor.

12. In the parking lot between the Tennis Club and the Ballpark, in Wolfscratch Village.

The Chapel

The growth of the Big Canoe Chapel has reflected the growth of the community as a whole. In the early 70's, Sunday services sometimes only drew a half dozen people during the winter months. There was no chapel, no community center. The worshippers met in a Treetopper, or a room at the Swim Club, or even outdoors.

Today, the Chapel is a major force in the community. It has built its own church, plus the Broyles Community Center next door. It sponsors a Boy Scout troop, is home to a Women's Guild, and is a major outreach force in north Georgia. It is presently building an ampitheater to hold 700 people, next to the Robert H. Platt Memorial Botanical Gardens just north of the main entrance.

The Chapel is set up as an interdenominational congregation that comes together to worship God and Christ. But it welcomes all residents and property owners, as well as visiting guests, of Big Canoe to attend its services and partake of its fellowship. It has a special category of membership for those who do not profess the Christian creed: fellowship member. As a result, a number of Jews, Unitarians, and even agnostics are members of the Chapel and help support its activities.

Bible, cross, and candles adorn Chapel's altar

The Chapel holds two worship services each Sunday in its sanctuary, which can hold as many as 350 people. The services are enriched by the singing of an 80-member choir, a men's chorus, the Big Canoe Chapel ensemble, and a hand bell choir.

But the ministry of the Chapel extends far beyond the bounds of Big Canoe. The congregation has been highly active in sponsoring and supporting benevolence programs, both locally and internationally.

"We have tried to carry forth the intent of the original Wolfscratch Village in helping prepare the youth of north Georgia for adulthood," says Administrative Assistant Charlene Terrell.

Bell Tower embraces Chapel entrance

Toward this end, the Chapel has been giving college scholarships to the youth of Dawson and Pickens counties for the past 20 years. During this time, more than 80 students have been helped to extend their education.

The Chapel also stands ready to help adults in these counties who run into hard times. But they do not just redistribute money. When an elderly woman in the area needed her stove repaired, but could not afford it, the Chapel stepped in and picked up the bill.

Each year at Christmas, the congregation "adopts" a number of families in Jasper and Dawsonville. Volunteers shop for the items on the families' wish lists, wrap them up, and deliver them to the chosen homes.

The Chapel's charity extends beyond north Georgia as well.

The congregation has been a strong source of support for a children's hospital in Brazil. In the years since they first began helping, the hospital has grown from a 3-room facility to one of the finest facilities in all of South America, treating more than 4,000 children a year.

"Our benevolence programs are very important to us," says Mrs. Terrell. "We are proud that for every dollar that is spent in operating the Chapel here, we give away more than a dollar in charitable support."

The third major focus of the Chapel is its role as "the heartbeat of the community," as Charlene expresses it. All kinds of clubs meet at the Broyles Center, which has large halls and a fully-equipped kitchen. Thirty-eight weddings were held during 1999 in the Chapel.

In fact, it was the energy of the members of the Chapel that first sold Charlene and her husband Dave on buying a lot and moving to Big Canoe. "I have never been involved in anything quite like the Chapel before," she says. "This is a rare group of kind and generous people."

The newest Chapel project, the ampitheater, is expected to be completed by summer. In fact, the Chapel is hoping that one of the maiden uses of the new facility will be to stage an outdoor performance of the Georgia Ballet Company.

New ampitheater takes shape in secluded corner
of Big Canoe just off Steve Tate Highway

You've Got Mail

One way to chart the growth of Big Canoe is to chart the expansion of Big Canoe postal service. When Big Canoe first opened, Big Canoe had its own post office—on the second floor of Wolfscratch General Store. When the population outgrew that facility, however, the POA built a separate building just up the hill for use by the postal service. At that time, the Big Canoe post office—a contract post office—was closed, and the new facility became a satellite operation of the Jasper post office. Mail is delivered to the individual boxes, but there is no window service. In order to buy stamps or pick up parcels, it is necessary to drive to Jasper.

The postal boxes in the Big Canoe post office are free to any Big Canoe resident who requests one. Applications must be filed with the Jasper postmaster. But the inconvenience of driving to Jasper to buy stamps has led many Big Canoeists to discover the post office at Marble Hill, just around the corner on Route 53.

Marble Hill is a full service post office. Many Big Canoeists also rent boxes there.

Nonetheless, the amount of mail delivered to the satellite post office has grown so much that it became necessary to expand

Postal worker Grecian Thacker pigeonholes the morning mail

118

The addition goes up; Katrina Holbrook at Marble Hill

the building. This spring, the POA undertook to double the size of the building to accommodate current and projected needs. The postal system will help defray the cost of the project, but most of the cost is born by the POA.

The Wolfscratch post office also provides bulletin boards for posting community notices and "intra Big Canoe" mail bins for exchanging letters and notices with other Big Canoe residents without paying postage.

The bulletin boards and mail bins are to be used for personal communication only—not commercial advertising. The bins are often used by the POA and HOA to notify residents of upcoming functions, for example. They can also be used to exchange notes with other residents. They are not to be used to distribute flyers soliciting business. The bulletin boards are to be used to announce events and to advertise items for sale by a home owner or lot owner—as well as to post lost and found notices.

Woodbridge Inn

When you are in the mood for "good food and plenty of it," the Woodbridge Inn offers it with something extra—some of the most engaging views in the area.

Chef Hans Rueffert says the Woodbridge specializes in "simple foods simply fixed," but the cuisine delivered to the table is never plain. It is painstakingly prepared in the rich tradition of American and continental cuisine—with a Bavarian touch.

Hans is the son of Joe Rueffert, who came from Bavaria in 1964 and took over the defunct Woodbridge Inn in 1976. He and his wife Brenda ran it as a restaurant only until 1982, when they opened up inn rooms in a building next door. That building burned to the ground in 1994, and was rebuilt. They have also added 6 rooms on the second floor above the restaurant,

Dining with the mountains in the distance

120

bringing the number of rooms in the inn to 18. But the central attraction at the Woodbridge is the food served every evening (except Sunday), and at lunch on Wednesdays and Sundays.

It is hard to imagine a more spectacular place to eat a meal than looking at Sharptop and Oglethorpe mountains through the spacious windows in the Woodbridge dining room. Directly underneath the east window is a lovely herb garden where the Ruefferts grow their own herbs. A few feet beyond is another, smaller "inn"—a multi-unit birdhouse for purple martins, which has always been well-patronized. In the distance are the mountains, including Sanderlin.

According to Hans, the most popular item on the menu is the rainbow trout, which they bring in fresh from Ellijay. It is deboned and sautéed in butter, then topped with smoked, whole almonds. It is an excellent presentation.

The "signature" meals of the house are the wild game and the roast lamb. Hans cuts, ages, and marinates the venison himself. The other wild game specialty is ostrich.

The rosemary roasted lamb is an exceptional dish. It is

Hans chopping onions

served in thin slices accompanied either by sautéed mushrooms or bearnaise. The bearnaise enhances the natural flavors of the lamb perfectly. Hans adds the subtle touch of thinly sliced Poblano pepper strips, which gives the dish just a touch of heat. The result is a superb entrée.

The veal also deserves special notice. More than anything else, the abundance of outstanding veal dishes on the menu confirms Joe's continental influence. The wiener schnitzel is

Joe tends his bromeliads

a particular favorite, but all of the veal dishes are prizeworthy.

The entrées are served with a roasted potato and a fresh vegetable—or, in the case of the venison, homemade German spaetzle and red cabbage. The Woodbridge also offers a variety of appetizers, soups, and fresh salads. The cream of Broccoli soup was smooth, tasty, and replete with tender chunks of broccoli.

But don't overlook the desserts. If you are lucky, Brenda will have whipped up a batch of her Georgia peach bread pudding. Some of the notable standards on the menu are the lemon cream pie and the hot fudge cake with pecans.

For those who wish to linger, you can order an excellent cup of coffee—or a variety of special coffees with liquor. The most intriguing was "The Pharisäer"—named after the Pharisees in the Bible. It comes complete with the story of its origins, in Germany. It properly crowns any dining adventure.

In visiting the Woodbridge, be sure to leave enough time, if the weather is right, to explore the grounds and examine the marble planters, a sideline Joe Rueffert has pursued since he opened the Woodbridge. Using slabs of marble mined in Tate, he handcrafts planters he sells in the lobby of the inn. The planters come with bromeliads and cacti he raises in his own greenhouse.

A marble planter

The Woodbridge Inn is located at 44 Chambers in Jasper—just across the wood bridge! Their telephone is (706) 692-6072.

Big Canoe Style

Even though all of the buildings and homes in Big Canoe use a limited range of materials and colors, to insure that they blend unobtrusively into their natural environment, there is still plenty of individualistic statements when it comes to architectural styles. It is possible to find just about every style of home somewhere in Big Canoe, from the rustic log cabins (some with million dollar interiors) to avant-garde contemporaries.

Some neighborhoods were deliberately built to emphasize a specific style. In Buckskull Hollow, for example, all of the homes are built with the tin roofs and front porches of many mountain homes in the South. In other neighborhoods, there is no set style, although most homes pay some kind of tribute to Southern traditions.

In fact, the floor plans and designs featured in *Southern Living* magazine are a very popular source for home designs and ideas in Big Canoe. They embody the quality and comfort most people living in Big Canoe desire.

A Chestnut Knoll home—the latest in Big Canoe elegance

Graceful lines distinguish this modern design

Contemporary stylings accentuate this home

Not all log homes are modest cabins

The stacked stone look of the 90's

Sconti condominiums

A popular Buckskull design

By the Book

What does a person who has worked all his life binding books do in retirement? Why, bind more books, of course.

Bill Fraker, now 75, bound his first book in 1942. During his long career, in Chattanooga and Dalton, Georgia, he bound thousands of books. He retired in 1987, after 45 years in the business. He and his wife Rosene moved to Florida. But when his son Jon and his wife Deanna decided to build a home a couple of years ago in Big Canoe, they asked Bill and Rosene to come live with them. They accepted the idea gladly. They occupy the terrace level of the home Jon and Deanna built.

It is a house with two garages—one for the cars, and the other for Bill's bookbinding. For Bill still loves to do what he has done all of his life.

Most of what he does is rebind valuable books that are beginning to fall apart at the edges—or even the seams. He might be asked, for example, to refurbish a family Bible. He will take it apart, straighten and jog the pages, resew the binding, craft a new cover—out of leather, if desired—and then attach it to the book.

Bill (right) and a co-worker examine second largest book

Other common projects for Bill include law books, diaries, and geneaologies.

On occasion, he starts from scratch. Not long ago, his sister produced a family history. She needed just a few copies, but wanted them bound. Bill obliged. He painstakingly sewed the pages together—he does all of the sewing by hand—and then attached a quality case binding to it.

To make the binding, Bill cut binder boards to size, then stretched bindery cloth over the boards. He composed the title and author's lines in hand type, and stamped them on

Bill uses his stamping press

the cloth in silver foil (he also has gold foil). He then used end papers to attach the case.

The final step was to round off the spine with a mallet that he uses for that purpose. "If you don't round them off," he explains, "They end up looking like a Sears Roebuck catalog."

The result: a hand-crafted volume in a perfect case binding.

Bill does not think much of the way modern books are produced. The cases are glued onto the book, instead of sewn. As a result, a hardbound can fall apart as easily as a paperback.

During his career days, Bill gained the distinction of binding what was believed to be the second largest book in the world—a directory of names compiled by the Lookout Mountain Museum near Chattanooga. It was three feet wide and two feet high, was ten inches thick, and weighed 286 pounds. He hand-crafted every aspect of the binding.

Bill charges $25 to $30 to rebind a normal-sized book. A family Bible tends to run about $75. They usually take four hours or more to restore.

The biggest threat to books? "Age," Bill says. "Sometimes the pages just start crumbling in your hand." But he has restored books published before the Civil War.

Architectural Control

Imagine Big Canoe with no architectural controls or covenants. Someone buys the lot across from you—the one with all the lovely, fully-grown rhododendrons and mountain laurel. They hire a builder from Atlanta who clears the entire lot of all vegetation, then builds a tract home with vinyl siding and a purple front door. When it is all finished, he puts in his standard $1000 landscaping package—a lawn, two saplings, and three privet bushes.

It happens all the time in Alpharetta, but it would be a nightmare in Big Canoe. Fortunately, architectural controls and covenants prevent this from happening. Although often misunderstood, these rules do all of us a great favor. They keep Big Canoe looking natural.

Bill White explains vista pruning

Most of the restrictions apply to the building process—and all construction plans must be submitted to and approved by the POA's Architectural Control Department before building may start.

All contractors are carefully screened to make sure they understand the need to adhere to the covenants in building homes. If they fail to follow these practices, future plans to build will be rejected.

"Most of our work is pro-active," Bill explains. "For instance, we encourage builders to save trees when clearing them, instead of just cutting them down."

Nonetheless, it is important that every Big Canoe homeowner and lot owner know about the covenants and guidelines and abide by them. Otherwise, they might unintentionally find themselves in trouble.

"We are not building inspectors," emphasizes Bill White, the head of the ACC. "Our role is to educate homeowners about the covenants and what it means to live by them."

There are three major ways in which the covenants affect residents, once their home is built:
• Remodeling.
• Restaining or painting.
• Landscaping, gardening, and tree removal.

"My advice is simple," Bill continues. If you are going to make any changes to the outside of your house or lot, give me a call first. I will let you know if you need to submit plans to us."

Take remodeling—as in adding a deck. It may be perfectly okay, but if it is not, you may be required to tear it down at your expense. Submitting a plan first and getting approval eliminates the danger.

Perhaps you want to clean up storm damage. The covenants permit it—but you may not re-

The sign above, stating that life in Big Canoe is "High Cotton," physically conforms to the design set by Architectural Control. Other designs of house signs are permitted, but should be approved by White's office. Signs can be commissioned from the POA's maintenance department.

129

move any flowering or fruit tree without permission. The prudent approach: give Bill a call.

The same is true with vista pruning. The covenants permit vista pruning to provide great views from your home—but only if an ACC representative is guiding the pruning. You may not do the pruning yourself.

Bill adds that his office is eager to work with anyone planning to repaint or remodel. "We keep records of every plan that has been submitted and approved for every lot. Let's say you need to refinish your house. We can show you what colors it has been stained in the past. Or perhaps you are planning to do some landscaping. We can give you a plat of your lot with topographical markings.

"We are not trying to prevent anyone from keeping their home in good shape or adding on. We just want to make sure that our guidelines are followed."

What happens if you see a neighbor with a chain saw cutting down trees? "Give us a call," Bill suggests. "If the neighbor has contacted us and asked for our approval, we can reassure you on the phone that the work has been approved.

"On the other hand, if he has not, we will contact him and explain the rules to him. It will then be up to him to correct the problem in accordance with the covenants."

Refusal to conform to the covenants may result in a fine—in some cases, as much as $3,000 per violation. "We try to avoid getting to that point," Bill said. "Most homeowners understand why we have covenants and cooperate eagerly with them.

"There are always those who think they know more than we do," he says, chuckling. "I explain that we have spent 27 years learning what colors and materials best blend into the surrounding environment.

"Big Canoe is an unique community," Bill adds. "It's not a metro subdivision. We live here in the midst of nature and wildlife. Without guidelines, we could easily destroy the one asset we all love. Observing these guidelines is an important part of being a responsible resident."

The End of the Trail

When the 2,150-mile long Appalachian Trail first opened half a century ago, it was about 20 miles longer. Its southern terminus, in fact, was on top of Olgethorpe Mountain, just to the west of Sanderlin Mountain. The peak—renamed from Grassy Knob to Oglethorpe after the founder of Georgia—has in fact been closed. It has been taken over by the Federal Aviation Administration and is used for airplane navigation. A marble obelisk to Oglethorpe, erected years ago by Sam Tate, will be cleaned up and moved to Jasper.

Vandalism caused the end of the trail to be moved from Olgethorpe to Springer Mountain itself a 8.5 mile hike from the closest access point, Amicalola Falls State Park. It is here that hikers embark upon the long trail, which follows the spine of the Appalachian Mountains all the way to the northern terminus, deep in the heart of Maine—or, conversely, conclude their triumphant journey and look for a good bath.

Primitive shelters are scattered every seven or eight miles along the trail, but there are no Waffle Houses along the route to slake one's hunger; the hiker must carry his or her own food and cook it on the trail. Nor are there hot tubs to soothe the weariness of tired feet, nor medic centers to tend to sprained ankles or other mishaps. It is a daunting challenge, but one that is accepted each year by thousands of people.

Oglethorpe, now home to the FAA

Amicalola Falls

If you are the rugged outdoor type, and occasionally pine for a slightly more difficult hike than the trails in Big Canoe provide, a great place to visit is Amicalola Falls State Park, just fifteen minutes from the north gate. Even if you are not all that rugged, the state park has plenty to offer.

There are, of course, the falls themselves. Amicalola means "tumbling waters" in Cherokee, and the 729-foot falls do precisely that. The tallest falls in the state of Georgia, they are a gorgeous sight to behold.

The state has done a great job in recent years in highlighting the falls. They have created a charming gathering pool at the base of the falls. From the pool, it is possible to view the top of the falls far above.

For a closer look, a new path leads up to a viewing platform which provides a much more intimate view of the cascading waters. It is a great place to sit and reflect on the power and spectacle Mother Nature provides.

The end of the Appalachian Trail is only 2,109 miles away

Other trails lead up to the top of the falls, where a bridge lets you stand directly over the tumbling waters. Be sure to stay on the paths, however; the rocks along the falls can be very slippery and dangerous.

The top of the falls can also be reached by automobile, and the park has conveniently provided parking.

A new feature is the "Hike Inn," a rustic lodge located five miles from the park on the trail to Springer Mountain and the start of the Appalachian Trail. If you make advance reservations, you can hike the five miles to the lodge, refresh yourself with a hot bath and a good dinner, spend the night in a private room, and then hike back the next day. The hike is rated as "easy to moderate."

The park sports a modern hotel with breathtaking views

of north Georgia—including Big Canoe. The hotel serves meals three times a day, typically a buffet. The park service also conducts regular programs on the plants, animals, and minerals found in north Georgia. These nature programs change from week to week.

There is a $2 admission fee for each car entering Amicalola. Entrance is free every Wednesday. Annual passes are available for those who wish to visit the park frequently.

Hotlanta

Life in the secluded mountain retreat of Big Canoe is made even more delightful by the knowledge that the metropolis of Atlanta is just an hour away. Whether you are a vacationer or a full-time resident, there will be times when you long for a day in the city. Atlanta answers the call.

Atlanta is actually a dozen cities clumped into a single metropolitan area of four million people. The city of Atlanta accounts for just one-tenth of this density—400,000 folks. Everyone else is scattered around this hub, from Alpharetta to Peachtree City.

Hartsfield airport, on the south side of Atlanta, is a common destination for Big Canoeists travelling to the city. The busiest

Kun Lun wrestles Yang Yang for door rights at the zoo

Sculpture highlights the flora at the Botanical Gardens

airport in the world, it is a convenient gateway to wherever you want to go. From Big Canoe, the trip to Hartsfield requires about an hour and a half down Georgia 400 to I-85 South, through downtown to the airport. If you are meeting someone, there is usually plenty of short-term parking. But if you are flying out, and need to park, it is best to plan on plenty of extra time. You may want—or have—to park off airport.

If your goal for visiting Atlanta is to see some sights, you might want to consider letting MARTA escort you. Drive from Big Canoe to the Perimeter Mall, just off the Dunwoody exit of Georgia 400. Park in the MARTA parking lot, then hop the next train to downtown. Many of the best attractions in Atlanta—including all of the major sporting venues—are accessible by MARTA.

Some of the key spots to explore would include:

1. The Atlanta Botanical Gardens, 60 acres of delight and interest just north of Piedmont Park in mid town. The gardens feature a conservatory, a gardens, and a woodlands. The most enchanting section are the gardens, where winding walkways lead you from one kind of garden to another—from a herb

garden to a rose garden to a Japanese garden, and so on.

2. Zoo Atlanta. Located in Grant Park, Zoo Atlanta is another oasis in the heart of urban congestion. Walking through the gate transports you to Africa and other wild locales, where the giant pandas and other animals will entertain you.

3. The Center for Puppetry Arts. Take your grandchildren, but go for yourself! This is a great place to visit even if they are not performing a show, which they usually are. Part of the center is one of the best museums in all of Atlanta, documenting puppets and marionettes from all over the world.

4. The Atlanta History Center is actually a campus-like complex in the heart of Buckhead, complete with the Swan House mansion, a plantation, and the center itself.

5. Fernbank Museum of Natural History explores the history and mystery of natural science, with all kinds of fascinating displays—plus an IMAX theater. It is just off Ponce de Leon Avenue in Druid Hills, on the east side of Atlanta.

6. If you want a day of Disney-type entertainment, take in Six Flags Over Georgia, located off of I-20 west just west of the perimeter. Take Georgia 515 from Jasper south to I-575, then I-75 to I-275 south, then I-20 west to the theme park.

7. The Fox is a wonderfully restored theater from the gilded age of the Roaring Twenties. The theater itself is well worth touring—or take in a show as well.

Two gorillas clown it up in a Puppetry Arts presentation

Walk 'n' Sniff

Want to take a different kind of hike? The trails of Big Canoe are excellent places for a "walk 'n' sniff"—a hike in which you try to discern as many different fragrances and odors as possible.

Since human nostrils are usually not very perceptive—or well-trained—it might be helpful to imagine you are a deer or a hummingbird. Can you detect the odor of danger? Can you discern the perfume of a flower laden with nectar? Or are you nonresponsive to anything other than a Big Mac at 50 yards?

The Nature Valley or the new McDaniel Meadows are perhaps the best places to conduct such a hike. If fragrant flowers such as honeysuckle are in season, their alluring aromas will be easy to detect. At other times, train your nose to sniff out the enticing scent of sweet shrub or crabapple. The fragrance of pine is always pungent and easy to detect—especially if one is newly fallen or cut.

Allspice

But beyond these scents, there are plenty of more subtle ones we should train our noses to behold and absorb. The cool fresh smell of Disharoon Creek running through the Nature Valley, purifying the air, is a good example.

Go where the butterflies and bees go. What attracts them? Keep alert for the scent of wild herbs—like Carolina allspice with its maroon flower and strawberry-pineapple scent.

Fill your imagination with these smells. It may take a number of tries to register a fragrance, but the effort is worth it. We can learn to inhale the secrets of the woods.

Just one word of caution: use common sense in sniffing out common scents. If you meet a little guy that looks like a black cat with a white stripe down his back, don't try to establish an olfactory relationship. Good ol' Pepe will give you a whiff you cannot walk away from!!

137

Indoor Critters

As a group, Big Canoeists love animals. Being able to interact with the deer and possums and geese on a daily basis is one of the main reasons many people decide to live here. But wild animals are wild animals, and we must never forget it. It is dangerous to start thinking of woodland critters as cute and cuddly. They are not. They live in the wild.

For that reason, indoor critters—also known as pets—are highly popular throughout the forest. Dogs and cats are the most popular, but songbirds and hamsters and other unusual pets reside here as well.

Joan Nelson walks Mick in Nature Valley

As long as the pets are indoors, there is no problem. But when they are taken outdoors, there are a few simple regulations to follow:

• Dogs must be kept on a leash at all times when they are outside. Because dogs need their exercise, Big Canoe has provided numerous wonderful places for them to romp and explore: McDaniel Meadows, the Nature Valley, and the track at the ball park, to name a few. But keep them on a leash, and under control.

• Make sure pets have all their shots. Wild animals can sometimes carry rabies.

• There are lots of vets in the area to care for your pets. For a referral, call Animal Rescue at 579-1026.

138

Animal Rescue

The love of a great number of Big Canoeists is evidenced in one of many community service organizations that have arisen in the last 20 years—Animal Rescue. Recognizing the need to care for and place stray dogs and cats, a number of like-minded residents got together in 1989 to form a pet rescue group.

They raised money through bake sales, yard sales, and by appealing for private and corporate donations. As the group expanded, so did their capacity to help the strays. At first, they worked in very primitive conditions. But for the past few years, the group has had its own facility near the north gate.

The trim little building houses an office, a wash room for bathing dogs, storage for food and supplies, and kennels for 8 dogs and 2 cats at a time. As animals are found—usually just outside of Big Canoe—and admitted to the shelter, they are examined by one of 5 volunteer vets from the area, given shots, and placed in a pen half inside the shelter and half outside.

Twice a day, volunteers feed the strays, clean their cages, and exercise them. On Sundays, the animals are taken to Pet-Smart for possible adoption.

About 200 animals have been rescued and placed since 1995.

The group has a web site at http://bcdogs.home.mindspring.com.

Volunteer Annelisa Green prepares a stray for exercise

Landscaping Nature

One of the great challenges to many residents of Big Canoe is landscaping. In the suburbs, landscaping is the art of imposing gardens, terraces, lawns, and bowers on a bare square of land. In the woods, however, landscaping must be more subtle. Nature has already provided the basic essentials—ravines, views, trees, and shrubs. The landscaping the homeowner adds needs to blend in—a personalized touch added to the canvas already painted by Mother Nature.

Tom and Barbara Ress built a weekend getaway on Ahaluna Place in 1991. After a few visits, however, they decided to move to Big Canoe permanently, even though Tom commutes every day to Northlake, where he is treasurer of Lanier International. When they built, they commissioned a small landscape company in Ellijay to draw up a plan that has now grown up into a

Barbara relaxes in her woodland paradise

secluded nest surrounded by mountain laurel and holly. "It is unbelievably peaceful here," says Barbara.

The Ress landscape enhances the natural beauty surrounding their home without intruding upon it. As a result, it won an award for "Woodland Landscaping" from the Big Canoe Garden Club.

Abiding by Architectural Control guidelines is very important in planning a garden. In general, only trees and flowers native to the area can be planted where they will be viewed from the road or other lots. In addition, strict rules control the removal of any tree or shrub from your lot.

The best approach: draw up a comprehensive landscape plan and submit it to the ACC for approval. Then you will know you are designing in harmony with nature.

Flowers enrich the view

A great place for a snooze

Whenever Barbara hears the ambitious gardening plans of a new Big Canoe resident, she laughs about "all-you-can-eat time at the deer cafeteria." She has learned to cultivate a "deck garden," planting flowers in pots where the deer cannot eat them.

The Tate Mansion

By the "Roaring Twenties," Colonel Sam Tate had consolidated the entire marble industry, and had become one of the richest men in America. He also had a huge supply of Etowah pink marble, a rare bright pink marble. One of his customers, an architectural firm, suggested that he build a home of this pink marble, as a showcase for his business. The marble was excavated in large blocks, which were placed on the facing of the home in exactly the same order and pattern as they had been cut from the quarry, so that the veins in the marble run from one block to the next.

The mansion was completed by 1926, and became the home of Colonel Tate, his brother Luke, and his sister Floratine.

It would be idyllic to report that the Tates lived happily ever after in their magnificent marble mansion, but such was not the case. Flora in particular became quite unhappy and reclusive. Engaged to be married to a local man, her brother flatly forbade the union. It turns out that the designated groom-to-be was in fact one of Sam's own illegitimate children! Flora never forgave her brother, and withdrew to an almost solitary existence in her spacious second-floor suite

A marble statue adorns the east gardens

Flora was the last of the three to die, and as there was no descendent interested in moving in—Steve and Lucille Tate were living in Big Canoe—the house was boarded up. This did not prevent scavengers from breaking in and looting just about everything of value during the 20 years the house sat idle.

In 1974, the house was bought by Ann Laird, who set about restoring it—no easy task due to the

decay and neglect. In Flora's final years in residence, for instance, a covert still was set up in the attic, and the whisky was carried out under her nose! When discovered by the revenue agents, the still was unceremoniously blown up, smashing a hole in the roof and causing mash to saturate the walls. All of this damage had to be repaired.

In its restored condition, the Tate Mansion was opened to the public and serves as a bed and breakfast for tourists and a site of historic interest. Self-conducted walking tours of the mansion and grounds—the gardens in particular are fascinating—are available for $3. Guided tours can be arranged for parties of 10 making advance reservations.

In addition, the Tate Mansion has been opening its dining rooms to the general public for Sunday brunch, and schedules dinner mystery theater presentations occasionally on Saturday nights. It is also a popular spot for weddings and other social functions.

The Tate Mansion is located on Highway 53 on the outskirts of Tate, Georgia. To schedule tours, call (770) 735-3122.

Sign Language

Big Canoeists are an expressive bunch of people. They sound off in many different ways. One of the most charming ways some residents make themselves heard is by attaching a phrase to the signpost in front of their homes. Signs must be inoffensive and in good taste. Here is a sampling:

Angel's Nest

Bearly Conscious

The Grand Escape

**Sans Souci—
No Worry**

**I Love
View**

**Me Jane—
You Welcome**

Recycling

The effort to renew our environment begins with our trash. Once upon a time, we dumped trash. Now, we dispose of it. There is a difference. Properly disposed, trash can be reused. If it is just dumped, it is worthless.

The POA maintains an excellent disposal facility for use by Big Canoe residents just past the North Gate. There is a trash compactor for any household trash that is "small enough to fit through the opening," as Toby Jones, who supervises trash collection for the POA, defines it. In addition, there is a large open bin where homeowners can dispose of "construction debris"—for example, old porch screening the home-owner has just replaced.

There is also a sequence of six bins to be used by those who wish to recycle bottles, plastic containers, papers, and cardboard.

"We encourage all home-owners to recycle their trash," adds Toby, "but ask that they be careful in plac-ing only the right materials in each bin. A plastic lid on a glass bottle will contami-nate all of the glass in the bin, once it is recycled."

For those who wish, trash pickup service is available, at an extra fee, from an outside contractor. Call the north gate for more information.

Jim & Linda Mullá recycle

Invading Chattanooga

Looking for places to take an occasional day trip from Big Canoe? Head for Chattanooga. Once you visit this town of song and movie fame, you will want to come back for more.

Thirty years ago, Chattanooga was named by the Environmental Protection Agency as "the dirtiest city in the United States." Now, however, the smoke and dirt are gone—and the city is vibrant, alive, and full of Southern charm.

It is also very convenient to Big Canoe. It can be reached easily in two hours by driving due west on Route 53 to Interstate 75, north to I-24 in Tennessee, and then west into the city itself.

Once you arrive, the place to head is the Visitor's Center at Broad St. and Second Ave., next to the Tennessee Aquarium. The good folks there can help you decide what to see. Many of the best attractions are within walking distance of the center.

Park your car and forget it for the day. Chattanooga is a town to explore on foot (they even conduct "Ghost Walks" after nightfall). Just a block from the visitor's center is the Tennessee River, and lengthy walkways stretch along both shores—and from one bank to the other. The Walnut Street Bridge,

The Chattanooga choo-choo ran to Cincinnati and back, and opened the first North-South railroad route

Cruising on the Tennessee, Lookout Mountain looms

Choo Choo Charlie

now more than 100 years old, is dedicated to pedestrian traffic.

The heart of riverbank activity is Ross Landing, named after Cherokee Indian Chief John Ross, who built the landing and a hotel about 1800. From Ross Landing, the riverboat *Southern Belle* departs several times a day on sightseeing cruises up and down the Tennessee. The cruise costs $10 per person; $16.43 if lunch is included, and $16 to $35 for a variety of dinner and entertainment cruises. The tour is enlivened by the friendly commentary of Choo Choo Charlie.

Walk a short way east from Ross Landing and you can visit the Hunter Museum and its wonderful collection of American art, with works by Thomas Cole, Winslow Homer, Mary Cassat. and Childe Hassan. Occupying the estate and grounds of a

Three centaurs cavort in Hunter's sculpture garden

Coca-Cola bottling executive, the museum outshines Atlanta's High Museum. In addition, there are several other art and sculpture galleries in the same block.

The star attraction, though, of downtown Chattanooga is back at Ross Landing: the Tennessee Aquarium. This is not just a big fishbowl; it is a four-level examination of the "story of a river"—all rivers in general, but the Tennessee in particular. Taking the escalator to the top, you are led from one fascinating display to another as you wend your way earthward. It is a truly impressive attraction.

Just to the south of town is Lookout Mountain, with Ruby Falls, Rock City, a botanical garden, and a battlefield. And there is more. In all, it is too much to squeeze into a single day. You'll just have to start planning a return trip!

Need a snack or lunch? *Cheeburger Cheeburger,* at Market and Second, makes great floats, and serves the *big one,* a one-pound burger. For dinner, try Rocky Top Café, across Second Ave. and upstairs.

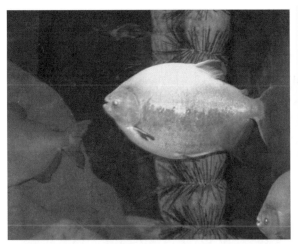

At the Tennesee Aquarium, from top to bottom: a pirapatinga, from the Amazon; a moray eel; and a smug show-off. To the right: a bird supervises the turtles down below.

149

School Days

As Big Canoe flourishes, more and more families with children are making it their permanent home. An important question for such families is: "Can my kids get a good education?"

The answer is an emphatic "yes." In fact, many families that have made the move believe their children have received a better education than they would have in a public school in Gwinnett or Fulton counties.

One great advantage is that the schools are not huge warehouses of children, as they so often are in the Atlanta area. Class sizes are small. There is more interaction with teachers. And the fierce competition among students in metro suburbs is almost non-existent.

About 100 kids from Big Canoe board the school buses every morning, half heading toward a Pickens County school and the other half heading toward Dawson County. Which school a child attends depends on where the family lives in Big Canoe, although Dawson children are allowed to attend Pickens schools.

Clayton and Lynn Burns and family, who live on Sanderlin Mountain, moved to Big Canoe several years ago to get away from the worries and stresses of big city schools. Clayton commutes to his work in Duluth, while Lynn teaches eighth grade at Pickens Middle School. Both of their children have been educated in the Pickens system—and done very well. Son Brady heads to Furman on a scholarship this fall.

"We have a very strong program," Lynn asserts. "The administration puts a heavy emphasis on reading skills at every stage of a child's education." Even though Lynn is a math teacher, "all teachers are expected to teach reading skills. It is a number one priority through our system."

Lynn also gives the school system high marks for innovation. A new approach to teaching math has just been introduced, she says, with great success. "I am teaching eighth

Pickens Middle School, looking toward Big Canoe

graders math concepts that I never learned until high school."

The middle school has a campus-like feel with a great view of the mountains. "It's fun teaching here. There is so much less stress than in more urban schools."

Lynn says what impresses her the most is the level of public support for the schools, both in scholarships and mentoring. Much of the credit for this, she adds, belongs to the strong efforts of the residents of Big Canoe, especially the Big Canoe Chapel.

"I could not believe the number of scholarships underwritten by the Chapel and other local organizations," she says. "It grows every year. " She said the Chapel has distributed eighty scholarships of $1,000 a year to students from both counties in the last 20 years.

Both school systems also benefit from the many Big Canoe residents who serve as mentors. "These volunteers make a great impact on the quality of education. We appreciate them greatly, and could always use more."

Mentoring, in fact, is just one of many ways to volunteer in the local communities. For more information on all of the volunteer opportunities available, contact chambers of commerce for Dawson and Pickens counties.

Smoke Signals

Every month, the latest news and notices about life in Big Canoe arrives, absolutely free of charge, in homeowner's mail boxes. *Smoke Signals,* as the community newspaper is called, is more than just a way of staying informed. It is a symbol of a community's determination to communicate with each other.

Smoke Signals is published by the Homeowner's Association and distributed free of charge to all Big Canoe owners. It began in the early days of Big Canoe as a eight-and-half by eleven-inch bulletin. As the population grew, so did the paper. Today, it is a 76-page tabloid filled with news, photographs, and advertising. It is a testimony to the economic strength of a small northwoods community.

Today's *Smoke Signals* is issued under the editorial guidance of Bennett Whipple, who works with a volunteer staff of journalists and photographers. Being an entirely volunteer enterprise, *Smoke Signals* has been something of an anomaly among newspapers. Staffers and stringers write what they hear about or find interesting, and it is published.

Bennett, who took up the reins of editor last fall, is trying to refocus the writing process to give it a more conventional newspaper format. "In the past," he explains, "the P.O.A. might send us the schedule for Fourth of July activities, and it would be run on page 37 of the paper. Now, it will be the basis of our lead story on page 1. It is, after all, the most newsworthy story of interest to our readers. Why should we make them hunt through the whole issue to find it?"

Another change Bennett is gradually implementing is to assign specific stories to his staff writers to research and write up. "There are plenty of people in Big Canoe eager to volunteer a column for us," he chuckles. "What we actually need are folks who are willing to write straight news stories."

Bennett says he is always looking for new volunteers to help with reporting, writing, and photography. He is striving to

Bennett Whipple prepares copy for an upcoming issue

present as broad a range of ideas, opinions, and interests as possible.

"We will print any article that is of interest to our readers," he says, "but we are not under the control of any group or faction. We are not the mouthpiece of the POA, the HOA, or any organization or club. Even though we are published by the HOA, we are left free to run the paper as we see fit."

He adds that his major goal is to make *Smoke Signals* more of a complete, well-rounded newspaper—and maintain its credibility as a reliable source of factual information.

The paper itself is produced by the staff of the *Pickens Progress,* and printed in Ellijay. All of the advertising is handled by the *Progress* staff; Bennett only has to focus on drumming up enough copy and pictures to fill each issue.

"The deadlines sometimes get a bit tight, but on the whole it is a real joy to edit *Smoke Signals.* I am proud of what our staff is able to do, month after month."

A Good Book

Love a good book? Looking for one to read?   Look no further—there are plenty of books to be found close by, both in Pickens and Dawson counties, at their public libraries.

The Pickens library is part of the Sequoyah library system, and can obtain any book carried by any of the libraries within their network.   Located just south of Cove Road off Burnt Mountain Road, the library is an easy drive from Big Canoe.

Although the library is not large, it has a geneaology room which draws people from out of state to research the past history of relatives who grew up in north Georgia.

Dawson County's library is part of the Chestatee library system, which also includes the Lumpkin county library in Dahlonega. Located at 298 Academy Avenue in Dawsonville, the library features a home delivery service for any homebound resident in Dawson county.

Both libraries offer internet access for any library user who does not have that connection at home. In addition, they have fully computerized card catalog systems that can be accessed by the internet from your home computer.

The Pickens library moved into a new building just four years ago; the Dawson library has plans to build a new library soon that will triple its space.

The Pickens County Library is just four years old

Coming Attractions

What lies ahead for Big Canoe? Since the best measure of the future is always the past, the best way to answer this question is to look at what Big Canoe has become in less than 30 years. In the next 10 to 20 years, therefore, we can expect more of the same—but better.

The task of leading Big Canoe into the future falls to three people—Bill Byrne, the president of Big Canoe Company, Bryant McDaniel, vice-president of development, and Nancy Zak, executive vice-president. This trio works full time to make sure that future development of Big Canoe unfolds properly.

"The future of Big Canoe was pretty much laid out by Tom Cousins when he first opened the development in the early seventies," Bryant observes. "We have not deviated from this original master plan in any significant way. If anything, we have found ways to implement it more effectively."

To illustrate this statement, Bryant points out that the current plan calls for a lower average density of residents per acre than the original.

"We have worked hard to preserve the original vision of Big Canoe," Nancy adds. "The intrinsic nature of the property is our most important asset. We guard and protect it accordingly."

Within this framework, development continues—and there are many exciting prospects for the future. The Big Canoe Company, in cooperation with the POA, recently embarked on a $5 million amenity package which will enhance the recreational opportunities at Big Canoe tremendously.

Part of the work, the development of McDaniel Meadows, is already completed. Work on the new swimming pool was finished in time to open as usual on Memorial Day. Work continues on the new fitness center which will adjoin the swim club. Set to be done by the end of this year, it will include an indoor lap pool, exercise room, racquet ball court, and more.

Work has also been started on the Wildcat Recreation Center, near the north gate. It's focal point will be an outdoor aquatic center. There will also be playing fields for soccer and other sports, a children's playground, and picnic and grilling facilities. A covered pavilion is planned for the future.

Big Canoe is just now planning the opening of the Wildcat neighborhood. The original master plan called for another 18 holes of golf to be built in Wildcat, but that idea has been modified. "Once we began seriously planning this area," Nancy explains, "we discovered that the topography, beautiful trout streams, and mountain ridges of the area offered a special opportunity. We decided to create a residential community with interconnected paths and hundreds of acres of green space that preserve the trout streams and spectacular mountain views."

As for longer-term development, Bryant says they have been working with the POA to create a plan for "reinventing" Wolfscratch Village. "We want to build walking paths and bike trails to connect the Sconti clubhouse to Wolfscratch and the ball park. We see this central core area growing into a more important focus for the community."

As beam is welded to beam, the fitness center rises skyward

Long-term plans call for development of an 1,200-acre tract of land across Steve Tate highway (running from the golf maintenance building to Route 53) called Potts Mountain. A new 18-hole golf course will be built there (designed by Joe Lee, the fairways were rough cut from the woods twenty years ago.)

In addition to golf, a conference center and inn is being considered. Residentially, there would be a mix of neighborhoods featuring single-family homes. "Potts Mountain has always been considered part of Big Canoe," Bryant adds. "Its development was part of the original plans."

Byrne Steps In

Tom Cousin's dream of a planned community in the wilderness of the north Georgia mountains began to take shape in the late 1960's. After acquiring the property, he set in motion the necessary steps: laying out a comprehensive plan, building the amenities, assembling the staff needed to maintain the property, and putting lots up for sale. Several years of exacting work preceded the grand opening in 1973, when hundreds of Atlantans flocked to Big Canoe.

Bill Byrne

Many of them bought into the dream, and the first homes started to sprout up. As people began to move in and take up residence, the first seeds of community began to appear. There was a great spirit of building.

That spirit was shaken in the last half of the 70's, as the economy soured. Interest rates soared to 20 percent. Housing starts dried up everywhere. Sales stagnated. Cousins could not sustain payments on his vast holdings. Something had to give—and the something turned out to be Big Canoe.

In 1978, Cousins surrendered his dream to the banks that had originally financed it. For 10 years, Big Canoe was managed and run by the banks. The sales team continued to sell lots, but with mediocre results. The ratio between resales and new lots was decidedly unhealthy.

The banks became dissatisfied, and began experimenting with ideas not in harmony with the original master plan—for example, time sharing. They also spent as little as possible maintaining the amenities. The roads and water system desperately needed attention. The banks then announced a plan to force the property owners to purchase the amenities under terms many saw as unreasonable. A group of owners formed the Homeowners Association and filed suits against the banks.

The suit was resolved substantially in favor of the HOA. While the settlement was being worked out, William J. Byrne bought—in May 1987—the development interest in Big Canoe.

Byrne saw that the potential of the community, and quickly began to re-establish a favorable image for Big Canoe. In 1997, he joined forces with Greenwood Development, a developer of resort and golf course communities. First alone, and now with Greenwood's backing, Byrne has worked to restore confidence in the value and quality of Big Canoe.

"In 1987, Big Canoe was a two-dimensional community consisting of a core of retired people and weekend vacationers," Byrne observes. "We now have a full spectrum community. More than 100 kids go to school each day from Big Canoe. Many permanent residents work in Atlanta—or telecommute. The average age of our population is steadily becoming younger."

As part of the acquisition, Byrne and the POA agreed that a percentage of the monthly POA assessments from each new lot sold and each new house built is set aside to fund new amenities. The resurgence of new lot sales in Big Canoe made it possible to add a third nine-hole course and an indoor tennis facility in the early nineties, as well as the $5 million package of new amenities now underway. The stronger sales—and the acceleration of home building—also strengthened the POA financially, leading to upgrades in the roads, improvements at the Sconti clubhouse, irrigation of the golf course, and expansion of the Canoe Lodge.

"In the last few years, Big Canoe has begun to realize more of its potential," Byrne says. "There is no question that, as big Canoe continues to grow, it will become the very special place it was envisioned to be."

It's A Snap

New editions of *The Enchantment of Big Canoe* will appear each year in July, as long as it stays in demand. One of our goals is to interact with the Big Canoe community.

Toward this end, we are announcing two contests for residents and lot owners of Big Canoe.

The first contest is a photography contest. The rules are simple: each resident or lot owner wishing to compete may submit as many as three photographs to be judged. The deadline for submissions is March 1, 2001. The photographs must be taken within the bounds of Big Canoe and must somehow illustrate the theme of "enchantment."

Photographs can be either black and white or color. They may be submitted in any size up to but no larger than 8 x 10. They can be submitted as prints or as digital files (Macintosh compatible). Photographs can be returned at the end of the contest, but only if you include a stamped, self-addressed envelope with your submission.

The winner will receive a $50 gift certificate to the Countryside Café.

The second contest will be a creative writing contest describing "the most unusual event of my life." It must be a true story; it can be retold in any kind of writing format you wish. This contest is also limited to residents and lot owners of Big Canoe. Entries must be typed and can run no longer than 1,000 words. The deadline is March 1, 2001. Entries will not be returned; be sure to make a copy for your own files. Entries will be accepted by e-mail.

The winner of the writing contest will receive a $50 gift certificate for dinner at the Woodbridge Inn.

All winning entries become the property of the publisher.

Entries for both contests should be sent to: The Pierian Spring, P.O. Box 271, Marble Hill, GA 30148.

Electronic entries can be sent to: c.japikse@worldnet.att.net.

More Enchantment

Individual copies of *The Enchantment of Big Canoe* cost $14.99, plus $2 for postage. They may also be bought at outlets around Big Canoe.

If you would like to buy multiple copies, in order to send them to friends and relatives still shoveling snow in Poughkeepsie or Fargo, we can help you. If you buy five or more copies at one time, sent to one address, the cost will be $12.50 apiece, plus $6 shipping. If you buy 10 or more copies, sent to one address, the cost will be $11 apiece, plus $10 shipping.

To order from the publisher, send a check or money order to The Pierian Spring, P.O. Box 271, Marble Hill, GA 30148. Or call (706) 579-1274 and charge your order to MasterCard, VISA, American Express, Discover, or Diners. You may also e-mail orders to: c.japikse@worldnet.att.net, or fax orders to (706) 579-1865.

Please add 7% Georgia sales tax with all orders.

Introducing: *Sophy*

The Journal of Inspired Writing

Sophy is a joy for people who love to read. Four times a year, we produce a new book chock full of stories, essays, and poems by great writers from the past—writers like Emerson, Poe, Thoreau, Wharton, Saki, Kipling, and many more! A one-year subscription costs just $36. Or subscribe for $64 and get the four books issued already plus the four being published this year—a real reading treat! To subscribe, write or call The Pierian Spring, as directed above.